Kiss of Death

On The Hunt, Volume 5

Samuel Davies

Published by S L Davies, 2024.

This is a work of fiction. Similarities to real people, places, or events are entirely coincidental.

KISS OF DEATH

First edition. December 15, 2024.

Copyright © 2024 Samuel Davies.

ISBN: 979-8227035066

Written by Samuel Davies.

Table of Contents

Prologue

G erard

The music pumped through my veins as I let myself go. It had been a hell of a year. I'd finally graduated from university and even got a new job. I was soon to be the first-grade teacher at Warrawong Primary School. I was nervous but excited. I took another shot and grinned at the bar tender, who batted his eyes at me.

"What are your plans for tonight, Tyler?" I hummed over the bar.

Tyler winked and chuckled. "I'm going home to my man. You know that, Ger."

I snorted and nodded. I'd been hitting on the bartender at the Pink Flamingo since I was eighteen years old and first came here. He knocked me back every time. Just like he did with every other guy that hit on him. Tyler was hot. He had muscles upon muscles, that silky tanned skin that I could see myself licking and eyes so dark that I swore I could be looking into the night sky. I reached down and adjusted myself in my pants. I needed some relief. I'd spent so long tied up in books and making sure that I kept my high grades that I didn't think about my dick. Tonight was different. Tonight, I needed the relief.

I turned and leaned against the bar as I scanned the dance floor. Men writhed against one another. A bachelorette party squealed and danced, bumping and grinding on the guys they had pulled into their group. A guy standing in his eye caught my eye. He wasn't what I would typically go for. But I wasn't looking to get married.

His black hair was cropped short all over. He wore an ostentation gold earring in one ear, and his jeans were impossibly tight. He watched the dance floor with interest, and I wondered if perhaps he had a guy here with him. Slowly, he moved his eyes over the crowd before landing on me. His eyes widened slightly before he schooled his face, and his lips tweaked at the corners into a small smile. I wiggled my fingers and licked over my bottom lip.

His smile grew, and he nodded his head. I pushed away from the bar and made my way toward him. The dark, handsome stranger kept looking at me as I moved seductively to him. Once I reached him, he looked me up and down and bit into his bottom lip.

"Hi there," I purred.

"Hello," the man said with humour in his voice.

"Are you here alone?" He nodded his head and continued to watch me with interest. "Do you want to dance?"

The guy shook his head. "I don't dance."

I pouted my bottom lip as I turned the brat on inside me. "What do you want to do then?"

He dropped his eyes and shrugged his shoulder coyly.

"Do you want to leave?"

"Maybe."

I smiled and moved into his space. I ran my fingers over his arms and felt him shiver. His hands gripped my hips as I pressed myself against him. Grinding my hardened cock into him. He growled low in his voice and leaned forward. He pressed his lips against my throat and gently nipped at the sensitive skin. I gasped, and my eyes rolled in my head as my dick jolted in my pants.

"Let's go to my car," he spoke quietly in my ear.

I moaned and nodded my head, threading my fingers with his and allowing him to lead me out of the door. I didn't know his name, but it didn't matter. This was going to be a one-and-done. I knew I'd never see this guy again. I just hoped he was good and would take that edge off that I needed.

He led me to a black SUV with the darkest tinted windows. It was parked in the shadows of the alleyway. Normally, I wouldn't even consider doing something like this. But my dick was doing the thinking. The guy opened the back passenger door and waved his hand for me to slide across the leather bench seat. I moved against the back driver's door and unbuckled my pants. Once the guy was in the car, he turned to me and bit his bottom lip.

"You want to suck me?" I purred.

The guy smirked. "Not yet," he said as he moved to crawl on top of me. Before I could even understand what was happening, a large tyre wrench came crashing down on my skull. My head split open wide, and I felt blood drip from the wound and into the collar of my shirt. My eyes rolled, and my head throbbed in pain and dizziness. I didn't even have time to cry out before another blow rained on my head.

Hit after hit pounded into my face and head. I cried and begged for my life. I was confused and didn't understand what was happening. How did a fuck turn into this? My brain tried to understand what was happening but couldn't work it out. Nothing made sense.

"Die faggot," the man spat as the darkness finally sucked me under, and I felt my heart beat its last. Death, I hoped, would be as sweet as my short twenty-one years of life had been.

Chapter One

Maverick

Groaning, I rolled in bed to switch my alarm off and rubbed my hands over my face. Frowning, I sniffed at the air. What the hell? Climbing out of bed, I slipped the boxers on the floor and entered the kitchen. The scent of coffee and bacon filled the air. I stopped in the kitchen doorway, and my eyes widened. Standing in a t-shirt and a little underwear was the cute twink I'd picked up last night at the Pink Flamingo. I was sure that he'd left before I fell asleep. Yet, he was cooking at my stove with Thor on the bench, watching him disgustingly.

"Oh, hey honey," the twink purred as he spotted me in the doorway.

I shook my head and frowned. "What are you doing?"

"I'm cooking us some breakfast. After last night's athletics, I thought we needed some sustenance."

Thor let out a long yowl, and I looked at my cat. I was sure I could see disgust written on his face. I never let my dates stay over. That wasn't part of the deal. I rarely brought anyone home. The rules were that we would spend a few hours having fun, but then they were to leave.

I shook my head. "That's nice, but why are you still here?" Hell, I didn't even remember his name. The twink's shoulders deflated, and I instantly felt guilty. "Look, I really appreciate that you are making breakfast, and I had a lot of fun last night, but I thought you understood that once we were done, you leave." I scratched at my chin as I remembered distinctly ordering him an Uber.

The twink sighed and nodded his head. "I know. And I was going to go. I guess, I just thought," he shook his head, and his cheeks tinted pink. "It's stupid."

I frowned and shook my head. "It's not. You thought maybe I would want more from you if you were still here this morning?"

He smiled and nodded. "Yeah," he laughed humourlessly. "See, stupid."

"Not at all. I get it. Let's have breakfast, and then I'll drive you home?"

The twink sighed but nodded his head. "I'm sorry that I overstayed my welcome."

"Don't stress. It's on me really. I don't want a relationship," I explained as he returned to cooking the bacon. I reached into the cupboard for Thor's breakfast. "I don't have time for one."

"Why is that?" he asked.

"I'm a cop. I spend the majority of my time at work. Last night was a rare night off for me. I never know when I will be called in for a case."

The twink's eyes widened, and he gasped. "Doesn't that scare you?"

"Being a cop?" I questioned. He nodded his head and flipped the eggs. I shook my head. "There have been some cases that I've worked that made me nervous, but not really."

"What kind of cases do you work?"

"Homicide. Although I only work on cases that involve serial killers or mass murders."

"You worked the school shooting?" he asked with wide eyes.

I winced and nodded. That was why I'd taken some time off. I needed a break after that case. It had really taken a lot out of all of us. So many kids were needlessly killed, and it all stemmed from bullying. The shooter had been broken and destroyed by bullies, and he did the unimaginable. It had been intense. The majority of the kids that had been killed were innocent bystanders who were caught up in the guy's rage.

"Shit. That would have been horrible."

"Yeah, it wasn't easy," I replied. "I'm sorry, you're going to think I'm a horrible guy, but what is your name again?"

The guy chuckled and shook his head. "I never told you my name, so I can't expect you to remember it."

I chuckled and felt my cheeks burn with embarrassment. I'd gone to the Pink Flamingo for one reason only. And that reason was standing in front of me. He was hot. There was no questioning that. And I could easily drag him back to bed for another round, but that would confuse the guy further.

"My name is Joaquin."

I grinned. "Well, I owe you some thanks, Joaquin. For last night and for the breakfast."

Joaquin snorted and handed me a plate of food. If nothing else, the kid could cook.

Chapter Two

H arris

I scratched at my belly as I walked into the kitchen. It was a rare weekend off, and I planned to take full advantage of it. I felt like my world had been a series of events for years. But with Daisy in remission and a lull in homicides, it was a great day to spend with my wife and kids.

Taylor sat at the kitchen table, tracing the edge of her mug with her finger as she stared down at the wooden table.

"Where are the kids?" I asked as I took in the silence of the house. It was never this quiet. The girls were usually loud, and at least one television would play Bluey or some other kid's show.

Taylor glanced up at me and gave a sigh. "At Mum and Dad's. I wanted to take some time to talk to you."

I frowned as something felt off in my gut. I pulled out the chair and sat down facing Taylor.

"What's going on?"

Taylor didn't meet my eyes as she sat opposite, staring into the cup of coffee, which looked like it had started to go cold.

"I can't do this anymore, Harris," she said after swallowing hard.

I frowned and shook my head. "Do what?"

"Us, Harris. I can't do us anymore."

My eyes widened, and I raised my brows. Where the hell was this coming from? I thought we were happy? In my mind, I'd never felt that we were in the wrong place. We would make love often, and even though my job kept me busy, I always tried to make time for Taylor and the girls.

"What do you mean?"

Taylor shook her head slowly, and when she looked up, I could see the tears in her eyes. "Harris, I've met someone else. I've organised a new place for me and the girls to live."

"What?" I gasped, unsure that I was hearing the right words. "Wait, who? Where? What?"

Taylor sighed again. "I'm sorry."

"How long have you been seeing someone else?" I asked quietly as the realization began to sink into my skull. Had I really been so out of touch that I didn't notice my own wife having an affair?

"A few months."

"A few months?" I shouted as I stood from the table, knocking on the chair repeatedly. "You've been fucking someone else for a few months? Letting me come home and pour out my heart and soul to you, and then what? Going to this other man and laughing at how stupid I am because I haven't noticed."

Taylor shook her head. "I've not been laughing at you, Harris. But I find it so fucking sad that I can have been seeing someone for a few months, and you are so busy that this comes as a surprise to you."

It was like she knocked the wind out of me. My heart ached as it tore from my chest. "Who?"

"It doesn't matter."

"Who, Taylor? Who? I should fucking know who?" I could hear the venom in my voice, but the anger was in complete control, and I wasn't going to be able to stop it. I'd never got angry like this, not with my wife. She had been the love of my life. We'd been together since high school. I never imagined that there would be something that would ever stop that.

"Jason Bourke," she answered quietly.

She might have punched me in the face. Jason Bourke, I knew well. Apart from Maverick, he was my other best friend. We didn't see each other as often as I would have liked because of work commitments. I couldn't believe the betrayal, not only from Taylor but from Jason.

I scrubbed my hands up over my face and turned my back. "I'm," I began. "I can't do this right now. I'll come back later and get my stuff. Don't worry about uprooting the kids."

Taylor said nothing as I stormed out of the kitchen to our bedroom. My mind was whirling with many questions, and I couldn't even think straight. All I knew was that I needed to get out of there. The temptation to go to Jason and kill him was strong. But what was the point? It wasn't going to make me feel better. As I slipped into the car's driver's seat and brought the engine to life with a roar, tears burned in my eyes. Disbelief, sadness and hurt were the emotions that filled my body. I didn't know what I was going to do. I didn't understand how she could do it. But at the same time, I understood it all too well. I was a cop. It wasn't unusual for a cop to lose his marriage because of the job. Our jobs were our mistresses. It was the price we paid for putting away the bad guys. I had always hoped that I wouldn't be one of the statistics.

Chapter Three

Maverick

I was considering taking Joaquin back to bed when the doorbell rang. I wasn't sure if I was happy or disappointed at the interruption. Joaquin deflated into the dining chair. I got the distinct feeling he knew he was wearing me down. I stood as Thor yowled. As I left the room, Thor turned to Joaquin and hissed.

"I don't think your cat likes me," he mumbled.

"He doesn't like anyone; don't take offence," I laughed as I went to the front door. Through the glass, I could see it was Harris, and he looked steaming. I didn't even get a chance to speak to him when I opened the door, and he stormed into the living room.

"She's been cheating on me," he thundered.

I stood in the living room doorway and blinked as my brain tried to catch up with everything.

"She's fucking cheating on me with fucking Jason Bourke." Harris thrust his hands into his hair and paced across the living room floor.

I gasped, and my mouth dropped open. This had to be a joke. Taylor was cheating on him. I never would have seen that.

"Mate, stop pacing, you're making me seasick."

Harris stopped, looked at me, and then toward the dining room door. I tensed and glanced over my shoulder where Joaquin stood with a pale face.

"I'm sorry. I didn't mean to interrupt," he said quietly.

I shook my head. "No. Sorry. This is my partner, Harris. This is Joaquin," I quickly introduced myself. I glanced around the room as I tried to remember where I'd put my phone the night before.

As if Joaquin knew what I was doing, he stepped further into the room. "Don't worry, I've already ordered my Uber," he explained as he waved his phone.

"Oh, thanks," I said quietly.

Joaquin smiled and looked like he wanted more. But what more was there to give? He quickly gave me a small wave and nodded his head. "I'll see you around, I guess."

"Yeah. I'm sure you will," I replied with a small smile before quickly leaning over and kissing him on the corner of his mouth.

Joaquin looked up at me through his lashes, and his cheeks tinted. "I'll go wait outside. I'm sorry, Harris, someone cheating is a dog act."

Harris nodded his head but remained silent. We watched as Joaquin left the house. Thor went to the door as it closed behind Joaquin and sat with his back against it as if he would keep Joaquin out.

I turned back to Harris and reached out. I pulled him into my arms and held him tight against me. Sobs bubbled from his chest, and his whole body shook under the weight of his cries. After a while, his sobs began to ease, and he lifted his head. He wiped his eyes with the back of his hands and groaned.

Harris sat on the couch and let out a long exhale. "I don't understand, Mav. What the fuck went wrong?"

I sat down beside him and frowned. "So, start from the beginning. What happened? How do you know she's been cheating?"

Harris sucked in a shaky breath, and I could see he was on the verge of tears again as he shook his head. "I was planning on spending the day with the kids, giving her a break," he laughed humorously. "She was sitting in the kitchen waiting for me."

"Wait, she told you in front of the kids?" I growled.

Harris shook his head. "No. Thankfully, she was decent enough not to have the kids around for that."

I breathed out a sigh of relief. "So, she told you she's been cheating?"

Harris nodded his head. "Yeah. She told me that she couldn't do the marriage anymore because she had been cheating on me with Jason for the last few months."

I frowned. It seemed like it came out of left field. Every time I'd seen Taylor, she was happy and looked at Harris with so much love. I knew he had been flat out recently, but Harris was there when Daisy was undergoing treatment. Hell, he spent more time in the hospital than Taylor did.

"What do you want to do?"

Harris shrugged his shoulders and rubbed his hands down over his face. "I don't know, man. I've got to find somewhere else to live, I guess. She said she had already found a place for her and the kids, but I don't want to upheave the kids."

"I understand. You can stay here. I've got plenty of room. And at the moment, you probably shouldn't be alone. That will eat you up even more than it already is."

Harris smiled over at me. "And get in the way of you and the pretty twink."

I snorted and shook my head. "That happens far less than you think. If he had gotten in the Uber last night when I ordered it, he wouldn't have been here."

Harris threw his head back and laughed. "Fucking hell, man. What the fuck am I going to do?" His laughter morphed into another batch of tears as he shook his head. "I want to call her a whore, slut, bitch, you name it, but I can't."

"No matter how angry you are at Taylor, you must remember the two little girls. She is still their mum. Listen, man, you make yourself at home. You know where everything is. I'm going to go and have a shower."

Harris stretched out and nodded his head. "Fuck, I slept like a rock last night, but I feel like I could sleep for another week."

"You've got the day off. Go sleep."

Harris smiled and nodded his head. I left him on the couch to go and shower. My heart ached for the guy. I'd always hoped to meet someone like Taylor, who loved me unconditionally. To know that she had been cheating on Harris shook me to the core. Was there any hope for true love?

Chapter Four

Killer

I stood with my back against the wall. The detective was here again. I smirked to myself as I thought about him. If he knew who was right by him. I watched him come every few weeks. He liked the same guys, twinks, young, pretty. I forced myself not to scowl and curl my lip.

Faggots. I fucking hated them. They were the scourge of society. It would have been fucking better without them. One by one, I planned to rid the world of them. A psychiatrist would probably tell me I was overcompensating for my own desires. My stomach clenched as I thought about it. I hated the urges. I hated that side of me.

I closed my eyes and took a large gulp of my beer. If I kept thinking about it, I would soon hear my father's insults as he whipped me over and over. All well-placed cane stripes over my dick as I sobbed and begged. I couldn't move away. I couldn't run. He had me strapped to the bed as he whipped me. I would promise and cry.

Anger rose in me with the images that flashed through my mind. I cleared my throat and swallowed the last of my beer. I needed to find someone. I needed to rid myself of the guilt. I wasn't gay. I didn't find men attractive. A real man didn't find men attractive. We didn't have sex with men.

I scanned the dance floor and looked back at the detective pressed hard against the twink who had his attention. I'd seen the kid here regularly. He was free with his body. I'd even seen him giving several men blowjobs in the bathrooms. It was fucking disgusting. I moved my eyes over to the bar where a man stood.

He was tall strong-looking, and even from here, I could see the desire in his eyes. I felt my dick give a twitch, and I balled my hands into fists and shoved them into my pocket. With a deep breath, I steadied myself and moved my way over to the bar. I stood beside the guy but didn't pay him any attention.

I waved to the bartender to get his attention, and he walked toward me with a smile. "What can I get you?" he asked.

"Beer, please," I replied with a shout over the thumping music. The bartender nodded and went to the fridge before bringing back the beer bottle and uncapping it with a grin. I passed him my money and returned to the dance floor once I had my change.

After taking a few sips, I glanced at the man beside me. He was aware of me. I could feel it. I could see it in the way he licked his bottom lip nervously. He was trying to gather up the courage to talk to me. I turned my attention back to the dance floor. I wanted to build the tension but not too much that he would lose interest and find someone else.

Up close, he was even more handsome than I had thought. He had blonde hair that curled around his ears. His eyes were a sparkling blue, and from the way that bottom lip wrapped around the bottle he necked, it was plump. Perfect for blow jobs. I frowned at the thought and took another large gulp of my beer.

I turned my attention back to the guy. This time, he turned to me at the same time and smiled.

"Hey," I said, leaning in close so I didn't have to shout.

"Hey, yourself," he purred. "What's your name?"

I shook my head. "Do we really need names?"

He bit into his bottom lip but shrugged his shoulders as he forced himself to look coy toward me. "How will I know what to scream later?"

I chuckled. "Call me Reuban." My name wasn't Reuben. I would never give my real name to those that I was planning to kill. I didn't want anyone to know what my real name was. I could never have done this work and been successful had people known who I was.

"Well, Reuben, how about dancing?"

I shook my head. "I don't dance, but what if we got out of here?"

The guy smiled and looked me up and down before he nodded his head. He turned to the bar and placed his empty bottle on the wooden top. I followed suit and then reached out to take his hand. Together, we walked to the exit.

"Have a good night, fellas," the bouncer said with a bright smile as we passed him.

"You too," I replied with a smile as I let my guy toward my car.

"Don't you want to know my name?" he asked.

"Only if you want to tell me," I murmured. In truth, I didn't give a shit. There was only one thing I was focused on.

"It's Michel."

"Great," I replied, trying to keep my excitement to a minimum. I didn't want to scare him away. I led Michel down the alleyway to where I'd parked. I removed the fob from my pocket and pressed to unlock the doors. I led Michel to the back doors and pulled it open.

"You want to do it here?" he gasped.

I chuckled and nodded my head. "We can do more later, but let's have a warm-up."

Michel giggled and nodded before eagerly climbing into the backseat. It was so fucking easy. Every guy was just so easy. They would always climb into my car without a second thought. No sense of safety. The only thing they thought with was their dick, with no thought to what might happen to them.

I slipped into the seat beside Michel and leaned over him. "Take your pants off," I whispered in his ear.

Michel's breath hitched, and he bit into his bottom lip. Slowly, he began to unbutton his jeans and began to slide them down. I took full advantage of his moment of distraction and lifted the tyre iron from the floor. Without a second thought, I swung the iron and slammed it into Michel's head. His eyes widened as the crack was recognised in his mind. He grunted, and his head fell to the side. I swung over and over as I felt the bones of his skull crush beneath the iron.

I let out a long groan as my cock exploded into my jeans. Slumping against the seat, I closed my eyes. My chest heaved with laboured breaths. I glanced over at the still body slumped against the back window. I smiled and closed my eyes again. I looked up at the roof and reached for the blood stain that soaked into the lining. Reaching with my finger, I used the blood to write the number eighteen on the lining.

I breathed out a long sigh. Eighteen dead fags. There seemed to be so many, but still a lot to eliminate. One night at a time. One day, I was going to succeed. My dad might one day be proud of me.

Chapter Five

H arris

I sat staring at the television that played quietly with Thor sitting on my lap. I stroked his fur and got lost in my mind. My heart felt like it had been torn from my heart. I wondered where it had all gone so wrong. What could I have changed? Would it have even made it any different?

"Here, man, eat something," Maverick said, breaking my stare off with the television. I glanced up at the plate of food he held out in front of me. I wasn't hungry, but I didn't want Maverick to think I didn't appreciate him. I took the plate and dug the fork into the potato chips before shovelling it into my mouth. It didn't taste like anything.

"I've texted Taylor. I will go over and pick up some of your stuff."

I looked over at Maverick and nodded my head. "Thanks, man, I don't even want to see her. I feel so disgusted."

Maverick nodded his head as he chewed his food. "I can understand that. I think you shouldn't speak to her for a little while yet. You need to process some of it all first."

I sighed and nodded. "I don't know if I'm ever going to be able to get over it. I just don't understand why. I didn't know what I did so wrong that it made her turn to another man. And to someone I actually thought was a fucking friend."

Maverick curled his lip over his top teeth and nodded his head. "I agree. I'm more disgusted by his behaviour."

I nodded. I was so angry. I didn't even want to begin to think about how I might respond if I saw Jason at the moment.

"Has he tried to contact you?"

I shrugged my shoulders. "I turned my phone off. I couldn't stand the thought of it."

"Probably a wise choice. He doesn't deserve your time. How much time saved do you have? Can you take some time off?"

I shook my head. I'd used all of my leave up with Daisy. In fact, I was pretty sure I owed hours. Besides, I didn't think I could take time off and get caught up in my head. Working would be a better place for me to be.

"I want to work."

Maverick chuckled. "We are alike in that. Work is my stress release."

I smirked and nodded. I knew that was the case. Every time life got too much for Maverick, he would throw himself even more into work. When his father passed away, Derek demanded that Maverick stay home.

Maverick's phone started to ring shrilly, and he lifted it from the table in front of him and frowned at the screen. "It's Xavier. Hello, what's up?" Maverick answered before listening to Xavier talk. "Hang on, I've got Harris here. Let me put it on speaker." Maverick pressed on the screen and placed the phone back on the table. "Alright, man, go on."

"Okay, so I've had a call from Jessie from Missing Persons. She has just taken another missing person report of a young guy, last seen at the Pink Flamingo."

I looked over at Maverick's, whose eyes widened. I knew that was one of his favourite haunts.

"Is it a homicide?" I asked.

"I don't know," Xavier answered. I frowned as I tried to understand why he was telling us. "The thing that caused Jessie to ring me was that this is the eighteenth man missing, last seen at the Pink Flamingo."

"Fucking hell," Maverick spat as he sat up in his chair. "And none of them have been found?"

"Not a trace. No activity exists on their accounts, social media, or contact."

"Why the hell are we only finding out about this now? How wasn't it flagged before?" I growled.

Xavier sighed. "Apparently, they had a system breakdown for a couple of weeks, and at least five reports went through different stations."

That made sense. But eighteen possible victims. We were going to be playing catch-up.

"Alright, get everything you've got on the missing men, and we will be in first thing in the morning and start going over it all."

"Thanks, guys. This one might be a bit too close to fucking home," Xavier growled.

I knew this one was going to be tough. His partner was a transwoman, and he frequented the clubs as well as Maverick. It made me nervous for both of them. Particularly Maverick, who often picked up on the nights he went out to the Pink Flamingo.

Maverick ended the call and sat back in his chair. "Fuck, man. This doesn't look good."

"Yeah," I mused. "You got any contacts at the club you could learn more about?"

Maverick hummed and nodded his head. "Yeah, I'll text them. I'll also organise to get any video footage. We are really on the back foot with this one."

I nodded. We often found ourselves playing catch up. It was time to shake off all the bullshit that my life had become and focus on finding these missing men. All I could hope was that we would see them alive.

Chapter Six

Maverick

Taylor opened the door with a sigh. She looked like she hadn't slept in a week. Dark bags were under her red-rimmed eyes, and her hair hung over her face.

"Hey, Mav," she said as she moved out of the way for me to enter.

Once inside, I turned to look at her. "Tay, what is going on?"

Taylor hiccupped a small sob and shook her head. "I didn't mean for it to end up this way."

"I don't understand. Taylor, you know that if you had just said something to Harris if you were unhappy, he would jump through hoops to change it. He would have quit the force if you asked him to."

Taylor sighed and moved into the living room before flopping onto the couch. A steady stream of tears trekked down over her face as she groaned. "I know. I'm an idiot. A slut, a whore."

I shook my head. "I don't think those things."

"I bet Harris does."

"No, I don't believe he does. He is hurt and angry, which is to be expected. But he loves you, Taylor. He loves you and the girls."

"I know he does, and I wish I felt the same way for him."

I sat down on the couch and glanced at her. "When did it change?"

She ran the back of her hand over her eyes, wiping up the tears that seemed endlessly flowing. "Probably a year or so ago. During Daisy's last bout of cancer treatment. He couldn't take the time off work, so I was left doing it alone. Jason stepped in and helped; I found myself leaning on him for support, and before I realised what was happening, I'd developed feelings for Jason, and one thing led to another."

"And you didn't think to speak to Harris about your feelings first?"

"Honestly, no, I didn't. It was stupid. I was so caught up in resenting him because I was doing everything here, running the house, taking care of Daisy and making sure Imogen didn't feel left out. I started to hate him, Mav."

I frowned and reached out my hand. "I wish you'd said something to me. I could have helped. Are you sure that you want to end your marriage? You could get counselling and work through things with Harris."

Taylor shook her head. "No. I don't love him, Maverick. I'm unsure how long it's been since I truly loved him. But it's been years. We got comfortable. We were going through the paces, and it was easy, but I didn't want it to be easy. I want to be in love. I want that feeling."

"But with therapy, you could possibly rekindle those emotions."

Taylor shrugged her shoulders and stared down at the floor. "Maybe." She looked up at me with brokenness written all over her face, and I knew there was nothing left to be said. She'd made her decision. "I don't think I want to fight."

I nodded and gave her a small smile. "Okay. Let me grab Harris's things. It would be best not to contact him for a few days. We've just landed a big case and will be busy."

Taylor laughed, but there was no humour in it. "Of course he will be."

"Taylor, you know it's not like that. He would have if you had told him to stop working at any stage. You know that."

Taylor sighed and nodded in resignation. "I know. That's what makes this even worse. I know that if I'd told him about how I was feeling a long time ago, he would have moved heaven and hell to change things. I hate that I've hurt him. I didn't set out to do that."

"I know you didn't. Just give him a little bit of time. Do the girls know what is going on?"

Taylor shook her head. "They are with Mum and Dad at the moment. I've told my parents what is happening but asked them not to say anything to the girls."

"I think that's a good idea. They need to hear it from you and Harris."

"This is going to crush them," she groaned.

"Yeah, it will. And you will need to ride through that. But I know if the two of you can keep the girls' welfare at the front of your mind, you will get them through it."

"Thank you, Mav. I'm sorry that I've caused all of this shit."

I smiled and squeezed her hand, but there wasn't anything I could say. She had made some horrible decisions. I hated cheating. I couldn't understand it. I'd never cheated on a partner, but I also understood how hard it was to be the partner of a cop. For cops, the job came first. There weren't a lot of marriages that lasted through this profession. Taylor and Harris's was just another casualty.

Chapter Seven

Harris

I'd barely slept and was grateful to be walking into the precinct. I'd tossed and turned all night as I thought about everything. I was driving myself crazy thinking about whether Taylor had fucked Jason in our bed. Had she come home with his cum still inside her for me to fuck her? I felt sick over the thought of it.

"Mind on the game, man," Maverick said as we walked into the precinct.

I nodded my head. The temptation to go and pick up to fuck around and make Taylor feel the way I did was intense. But I knew that wasn't going to make me feel better. I needed to move through it. I just wished it would happen sooner rather than later.

"Hey, Xavier," Maverick greeted as we went to the homicide cop's desk.

"Hey guys, I'm glad you're here. This is a bit of a mind fuck."

I sat down opposite and pulled the files over to me. I flipped open the folder on top and scanned over the information. Gerard Lopez reported missing last year after a night out at the Pink Flamingo. Since that Saturday night, he hadn't contacted his family and friends.

I frowned as I scanned the page. No one saw him leave the Pink Flamingo. He disappeared without a trace.

"That's the first one I can find that was reported missing from the Pink Flamingo," Xavier explained. "I contacted Stephen Cartwright, the guy that reported him missing. Apparently, Stephen and Gerard were housemates. Stephen hadn't thought of Gerard not coming home after a night out, but when he didn't turn up for his first day at work, he made the report."

"What precinct was he reported to?" Maverick asked.

"Footscray," I answered. "Have they all been reported missing from different precincts?"

Xavier nodded. "Yeah, mostly. We've had one other than Michel here, Koby Lewis. Then Footscray had Gerard and Kai Green. Three were reported at St Kilda, Feliz Anes, Cameron Thomas and Luca Bahl. Mason McGrath was reported at Geelong. Spencer Robinson and Eli Elliot were reported missing at Dandenong. Ryder Monson was Richmond, and Christian Spielman was Preston. Tom Schuster, Marc Brendal and Chaitan Sorcar were reported to Nunawading. Arpan Kivaraj was the furthest away he was reported missing in Shepparton, but I've included him because his last known was the Pink Flamingo."

I sighed. "That's a lot of guys."

"Yeah, and they all seem to be different nationalities. The only thing they have in common is the Pink Flamingo," Maverick said as he leaned back in the chair and scratched at his chin.

"That alone is weird. Serial killers usually have a type, not a place."

"Yeah," Maverick agreed.

"Do you think it is a hate crime?" Xavier asked.

Maverick hummed and nodded his head. "It's possible. But none of their bodies have turned up?"

"That's what I was just researching. I was going through all the Johns we have on file."

"Any luck?" I asked.

Xavier waved his hand. "Possibly. There have been a bunch of body parts that have shown up in a lot of different places. None of the intact bodies match our missing guys, but it is possible that some of the body parts could be them."

I scrubbed my hand over my face. That would make it even harder. "Alright, well, this is going to be fun," I groaned.

Xavier chuckled. "Yeah, we've got a curly one now."

"Let's start with the missing person files. How long is there between each report?"

"Two weeks. To the very day," Xavier answered.

"Okay, that tells me there is something suss," I mused.

"Yep, that was what flagged for me, too," Xavier answered.

"I'm going to go and talk to Derek, Xav. I think we are going to need you with us on this one," Maverick said as he stood from the chair and went to walk into Derek's office.

"Harris, are you okay? You don't seem yourself today," Xavier asked quietly.

I gave him a small smile and nod. "I can't talk about it now, but it will all work out in the end."

"Daisy?"

I shook my head. "No. She is healthy, thankfully. Just life."

"Alright, man, I'm here if you ever need a shoulder."

"Thank you, Xavier, which means a lot."

Chapter Eight

Killer I leaned against the side of my car and closed my eyes. Blood dripped from my cheeks, and sweat coated my brow. This was the part I hated. The adrenalin was gone, and the kill was complete. Now, it was about discarding the body. It was hard work and messy. I hated both. I looked down at the pile of limbs that sat at my feet. With a sigh, I grabbed the leg and threw it over the bridge, followed by the arm and torso. Blood pooled in the bottom of the tarp that I'd laid the body parts on to move them to the dumping ground. I didn't have a particular place where I liked to dump the body parts. Any place would do. As long as it was somewhat secluded. It wasn't about hiding them well. It was more about just not getting caught in the process.

I threw the last arm over the side of the bridge and looked down at the body parts scattered over the dry creek bed beneath. They would start to stink by the morning, and I had no doubt they would be found by foxes and crows. If I was lucky, the animals would get rid of all the meat before the cops found the body.

I didn't live for the infamy. It wasn't why I did any of this. My murders were only to rid the world of a disease that seemed to be spreading faster than I could. I lifted the tarp and threw it down over the bridge. It got caught in an old straggled tree on the side of the creek bed and waved around like a freak flag.

I looked over my car to ensure I'd picked up everything I needed and wasn't leaving anything behind. Climbing into the driver's door, I brought the car to life and pointed toward home. I pulled the car round the back of my house. Not that I really needed to worry. I lived far enough out of the nearest suburb that I didn't have close neighbours. It was the house I'd grown up in. The one that brought more pain than it did pleasure. But it was mine, and it was comfortable enough.

I wasn't a materialistic man. I didn't care to have a mansion or fancy gold taps on my bath. I just needed a small house, my dog and a bed to sleep in. That was enough for me. I climbed out of the car and chuckled as Rollo came running up to the side of the vehicle. He sniffed at the doors and licked at the spatter of blood that was on the passenger door. I'd wash it in the morning. I scratched at his ears and whistled as I walked in through the back door. Tossing my keys onto the kitchen table, I stripped off my jeans and shirts and kicked my boots to the side. Once my clothes were in the washer, I walked through the house naked until I reached my bathroom and flipped the taps on in the shower.

Steamy hot water streamed down, and I stepped in under the heat, feeling it soak into my muscles. Closing my eyes, I lifted my face to the stream and let exhaustion wash over me.

I hadn't seen a single report about the missing men. I had wondered at first if it were a case they hadn't been missing. Maybe their families had been like mine, perhaps once they realised the disgusting things the men liked to do in the dark was enough to turn their back. But I knew that couldn't be the case for all of them. There had to be some that were missing their sons.

My mind moved over the faces of the men whose lives I'd ended so far. It wasn't as many as I would have liked, but it was enough to make a dint. I knew that I wouldn't end it ultimately. That was impossible, and the way that the world was going, there were more that were turning to sexual deviants. It was fucking disgusting.

I scrunched my nose sand snarled as my cock gave a kick at the thought of being with another man. I fucking hated that part of me. I was no faggot. My father had seen to that. I reached around my back and fingered the raised scars dotted along the skin. He'd caught me masturbating to a gay porn magazine I'd found at the back of a shop one day. He'd dragged me out of the house with my pants still around my ankles. He had a fistful of my hair as he pulled me to the tool shed.

"Lay over the bench," he snarled, pushing me against his workbench. I'd never been so scared in all of my life. "No son of mine will be a fag."

Before I could even catch up with what was happening, the cane snapped over and over against my back. I remembered screaming and begging for his forgiveness, but he would hit me again and again. After that, I promised that I wouldn't be gay. I told him that I was straight. The following day he'd hired a prostitute and sat in the living room watching me fuck her. It was the most humiliating thing I'd ever been through. I couldn't even get hard. But like the threat of more violence scared me more, I urged my dick to get hard enough to fuck the woman.

After that, he continued to remind me that I wasn't gay. That was disgusting. I opened my eyes and looked down at my body. I had been disgusting. But now I was making amends. I was going to end the lives of other disgusting men. I was going to rid the world of faggots. One by fucking one. I would end them.

Chapter Nine

Maverick

I rapped my knuckles on the door jamb to Derek's office and waited for him to look up. He smiled and waved me in. I entered the office and turned to shut the door behind me. When I turned around, Derek watched me with his brows raised.

"One of these meetings?" he questioned.

I chuckled and shook my head. "Look, it's not all bad. I just wanted to discuss a few things with you. Harris will probably come and speak to you soon, too, but I wanted to inform you that he will likely be throwing himself into work pretty full-on over the next bit."

Derek's brows pinched into a frown, and he shook his head. "Why?"

I breathed in deeply and slowly let it go. "He and Taylor are having some trouble. I won't go into it, but I've told him to come and speak to you."

Derek nodded his head. "Okay, thanks for the heads up. Do you think it's going to affect his work?"

I shook my head. "No. I don't think so. The other thing I wanted to discuss was this case that landed on Xavier's desk, the missing men from the Pink Flamingo."

"Ah yeah, I'd wondered if we were looking at a serial case."

"Yeah, it appears to be," I said as I folded my arms. "We haven't got bodies I know of yet, but I'd like Xavier and Harris to work with me on this. Xav is also a frequent visitor to the Pink Flamingo, so I think he will be a good set of eyes to have on it."

Derek hummed and nodded. "Yeah. But if something comes up, I will have to pull him away. I'm short-staffed in homicide at the moment. April started maternity leave, and Brice is on light duties."

"How long has April got left?"

"Any day now," Derek chuckled. "Nara has been baking up a storm to take meals over there when the baby arrives, so she and Jamie don't have to worry about cooking."

I smiled. "You married a good one."

Derek's grin was wide as he nodded his head. "Do I ever." A knock sounded on the door, and when I turned, I saw Harris poke his head in. "Hey Harris, come on in. We are discussing Xavier partnering with you and Maverick on this case."

Harris stepped into the office and forced a smile to his lips. I could read it all over his face. He was miserable. Only time was going to heal it, and it wasn't going to be easy.

"Yeah, what's the verdict?" he asked.

"I said I was happy for it unless something arises that I need extra homicide for."

"Great," Harris answered as he fidgeted with his fingers. "Listen, Derek, can I chat with you briefly?"

"Sure, have a seat," Derek replied. I squeezed Harris's shoulder as he sat before the captain and ran his hands down over his pants.

"I'll go and make some contact with Dean and ask about those body parts we've had turn up."

Derek smiled and nodded as I walked out of the office and shut the door behind me. Although I knew Harris wouldn't have cared if I remained in the office, I felt it was probably better for him to talk to Derek alone. Derek had better insight into relationships than I did. I'd never had a wife or a husband. I'd never let my guard down long enough to want to get into a relationship.

"I'm going to ring Dean to find out what he knows about the body parts that have turned up and gone through his office. Do you want to pull all the other files that have happened in the time that our missing men have been reported? We can go through the others," I said to Xavier as I reached his desk.

"Already on it," he replied with a grin.

I chuckled, slipped my phone from my pocket, and scrolled through the contacts for Dean's number.

"Dean Richards," he answered on the second ring.

"Hey, Dean, it's Mav. I want to lend your brain a little bit if I can."

"Sure, what's up?"

I explained to Dean about our missing person's cases and the connection that could be found between John Doe's and body parts.

"I can't see that it would be one of the John Doe's because we always run their face through the missing persons database, but the body parts are more probable. The issue is finding which body parts belong to which missing man."

I hummed. "Any distinguishing features could definitely help."

"Yeah, we run that too, so if there was a tattoo or something like that, we would have been able to match it to the missing person. Unless the people making the report didn't know about a tattoo, scar, or anything like that."

"The only way we could really be able to give a definite answer would be through DNA, right?"

"Yeah, that would be ideal. If you could find the closest blood compared to the missing person or something with recent DNA, like a recently used toothbrush, we could match them. It would take a few months for DNA to come back, though. We've got a backlog at the moment."

Damn, that wasn't what I wanted to hear. Not to mention, it would be like finding a needle in a haystack. Especially if we had to test every body part.

"Alright, thanks, Dean. Leave it with me. I'll probably have more to talk to you about later."

"No problems." Dean ended the call, and I walked back into the homicide office just as Harris came out of Derek's office. I nodded to him, asking silently if he was alright. Harris smiled and gave me a slight nod of reassurance, and we joined Xavier back at his desk.

"Dean says that they would have checked all tattoos and markings, but I think, seeing as there was a database breakdown over the last few weeks, we should go back and start there," I said as I sat beside Harris.

"That's a good idea," Xavier said as he separated the files and handed us each a pile.

I grabbed the folders and walked into the serial killer unit room and to my desk before firing up my computer. Harris joined me and sat at his desk.

"All good?" I asked as I waited for the laptop to load.

"Yeah, Derek understands. He offered me time off, but I'd rather work."

I smiled and nodded. It wasn't my place to say anything. Hell, I couldn't really say anything; I was no different. I worked when I was stressed. It was how I coped.

Chapter Ten

Harris

"You look like someone pissed in your cornflakes," Derek said once the door shut behind Maverick.

"I feel like I've been run over by a steamroller," I answered as I sat before my boss.

Derek nodded. "Talk to me."

I scrubbed my hand up over my face. "Taylor told me yesterday that she has been cheating on me for the last few months with my best friend."

"Mav?" Derek growled, his face suddenly looking thunderous.

I shook my head. "No. Jason Bourke."

"Ah, okay, I don't know him."

"He is a paramedic."

"So, what is going to happen?"

I shrugged my shoulders. "I don't know, to be honest. Taylor said that she was going to move out of the house. But I told her to stay. I don't want to uproot the girls. This is going to be hard enough on them. I'll move out, and then we will face a divorce."

"Alright. I suggest you get yourself a lawyer," Derek said, waving his hand before I could protest. "It's not to make things difficult for Taylor but to cover yourself. While she might not seem nasty about things, this is new territory."

"Yeah, you're right. I never thought she'd cheat on me."

"That's right. Speak to a lawyer and find out what process you need to follow. You will also need to sort something out about custody of the girls. I'm assuming you're happy for them to stay with Taylor?"

I shook my head. "I guess so. I hate that Jason will father my daughters, but I don't have the time to be a full-time father."

Derek nodded his head. "That's right. Take it one step at a time. Being a cop does make a marriage difficult to maintain. Being a homicide detective is even worse. We don't get the opportunity to put our families first, and not all marriages survive that."

I knew that Derek was divorced; he had his partner now, but before he met her, he had already been divorced once. This fucking job. I loved it and couldn't imagine doing anything else, but it destroyed and took everything I loved. Tears burned in my eyes as I thought about Taylor. Of all the people that I never thought would betray me, she was the one. I loved her so fucking fiercely, and she had managed to completely destroy my soul.

"Do you need to take some time off?" Derek asked.

I shook my head and wiped the back of my hand over my eyes, leaking stray tears. "I can't. I'll get all caught up in my head, and I won't be able to think of anything else. I need to stay busy."

Derek nodded. "I understand that, but if I see this is starting to affect your job, I will pull you off."

I nodded. "Thank you." I stood from the desk and went to the homicide room, where Maverick sat before Xavier.

Maverick handed me some folders, and I started to flick through them. I needed to get my mind back in the game. I couldn't focus on Taylor and what she was doing. It was hard to think about. Was she fucking him now? Where were the girls when she fucked him? Was it in our bed? Did she come home from him and then make love to me? My stomach clenched, and nausea washed over me. The thought of being touched while the feel of his dick was still in her was horrifying.

"Want to read me out the names and any identifying marks so I can input it into the database to see if we get a match?" Xavier asked, drawing my attention to him.

When I looked up, I could see the knowing look he had in his eyes. He knew I wasn't okay, but he would let me tell him at my own pace. That meant more than I could express.

I nodded and glanced at the first folder. "Okay, I've got Gerard Lopez, twenty-one. He had a tattoo of a lion on his upper right abdomen and a hook tattoo on his left arm."

Xavier typed into the system and scanned through the information. "Bingo. We have an arm with a hook tattoo but no lion on the abdomen. Do we have a picture of the hook?"

I shook my head and placed a sticky note on the folder. "He has a brother as a contact here. I'll give him a ring to see if we can get a photo of the hook or if he can identify the tattoo."

Xavier nodded his head. "Good idea. Okay, next?"

Chapter Eleven

Maverick

After going through our list, we were able to put a few of the body parts potentially with our missing men.

"Ready to go out to visit, Louie?" I asked as I slid into the seat beside Harris, who was frowning at the file.

"Hmm?" he mused as he looked at me.

"Louie? Gerard's brother, ready to go and meet him?"

Harris shook his head and then nodded. "Yeah, sorry, I thought all these body parts matched none of the missing men. Who dropped the ball?"

I shrugged my shoulders. "I don't know. We need to go and speak with Harley. Maybe he can let us know how they missed it. Or maybe it is just because the body parts were found in different precincts to where the missing report was done."

"Yeah, but it should have been flagged in the system."

I shook my head. "Only if someone is actively looking. We have to match them manually."

Harris sighed. "Yeah, I guess so. Are we going to Louie's house?"

I shook my head. "No, Jennette said he was downstairs waiting for us."

"Okay," Harris answered as he stood and gathered the pictures of the tattoo, which we would hopefully use to be able to find Gerard. Dean said we could use Louie's DNA to match the other potential body parts. This was the more laborious part of dealing with this sort of case. It wasn't like it was on television, with every case solved in an hour. We could be working on this over the next year. I hoped we wouldn't be. I didn't want to think about how many other bodies would turn up. We needed to find the killer fast.

I knocked my knuckles against the door and entered the interview room. A dark-haired man sat in a chair, bouncing his leg up and down.

"Hello, Louie, my name is Detective Maverick Wolfe, and this is my partner, Detective Harris Bishop. Thank you for coming down."

Louie looked up and gave me a small smile. "You said on the phone that you might have information about Gerard?"

I nodded and sat opposite Louie while Harris took the other seat. "We have been asked to come on board to investigate a series of missing persons from the Pink Flamingo. Gerard's name came up in our investigations as that was the last place he was seen."

Louie winced and nodded his head. "I take it that you didn't approve?" Harris said.

Louie sighed. "It's not that I disapproved. I worried about him. He was a good kid. He'd worked hard at university and got a great job that he was meant to start. But he was dumb as well. He trusted too easily and was too free with his body. I was always afraid that one day, someone would take advantage of him and hurt him. And now," Louie let the statement hang in the silence.

I nodded my head. "I'm sorry that this has happened, and I'm hoping to be able to show you a photo of a tattoo to see if this was Gerard's."

Louie nodded and leaned forward in the seat as I opened the folder and turned the photo of the arm with the hook tattoo. A groan fell from Louie's lips, and he hiccupped a sob. I took the image back and placed it into the folder.

"Is that Gerard's tattoo?"

"Yes," Louie sobbed. He leaned forward in his seat and buried his face in his hands as long wails fell from his lips. My heart ached for the guy. This was always the most challenging part of being a homicide cop. Breaking the news to the families was never pleasant. All of their pain was evident, and there was nothing I could do to make it better. "He's dead?"

I nodded my head. "Yes. If that is his tattoo, then yes, I'm sorry, Louie, but he has been murdered. If you are willing, I would like to take a DNA swab from you to cover all bases to ensure the body belongs to Gerard."

Louie frowned but nodded his head. "Of course. But that photo. It was his arm only."

"Yes."

"Have you. I mean, it is there. Have you found his other body parts?"

"We have found other parts of his body, but I can't say with absolution that all the parts are there. His body was found a year ago, and only now are we putting the two together."

Louie's eyes widened, and he gasped. "How? How was it not found that he was the one."

"I don't have a definitive answer for you on that. All I can say is that I believe it is because Gerard was reported at one precinct, and his body was discovered in another precinct, and there has been a lack of communication."

Louie's eyes hardened, and he tightened his jaw. I could see his mind working and knew he wasn't happy about the information. He had spent a year wondering what happened to his brother, and the whole time, the body parts were being kept on ice. There was a definite issue, but that was above my pay grade. All I could do was connect the dots now and hope that we found the killer before there were too many other murders.

Chapter Twelve

Harris

I felt awful for Louie, who sobbed. I wished I could have changed it for him. Something about finding his brother's body in bits and pieces made it worse. What Louie didn't realise was that some of the body was still missing. There was going to be no open casket. None of the bodies had their heads. It was gruesome.

"Let's go and take this over to Dean," Maverick said as he waved the DNA we'd collected from Louie. "Xav will go and speak to some of the other guys' other family members. And then I want to go to the Pink Flamingo and chat with Tyler."

I nodded, followed Maverick to the car, and slid into the passenger seat. "Who is Tyler?"

Maverick snorted. "He is the bartender. If anyone is going to notice the missing guys, it is Tyler."

"And is Tyler a favourite?" I asked with a raise of my brow.

Maverick barked out a laugh and shook his head. "No. Tyler doesn't go home with any of the patrons."

I nodded my head. "Are you happy?" I asked suddenly.

Maverick glanced over at me and raised his brows. "Yeah? Where is that coming from?"

I shrugged my shoulders. "I don't know how to be single. I wondered if you were happy or wanted a relationship."

Maverick hummed. "Sure, I'd like a relationship one day. But I also recognise that my life isn't conducive to a successful relationship, so I don't want to put someone through that."

It was like he'd slapped me. I blinked and sat back in my chair. "I've been a selfish prick," I mused.

Maverick shook his head. "Taylor knew what she was getting when she married you. The two of you had been together since high school. She supported you in becoming a cop. Remember, you didn't want to advance higher than uniform, but Taylor pushed you to take the promotion."

I nodded. It was true. Taylor had talked me into it because it meant a higher wage. I'd argued with her that it wouldn't be suitable for the girls that I wouldn't be home as often, but she told me that she was prepared for that. She hadn't been. I scoffed and shook my head. I couldn't help but wonder how many other fucking lies she'd told through our marriage.

"Listen, Harris, what Taylor has done to you is fucked. It's a shitty thing, but please don't let it turn you bitter. I understand; you're angry and hurt and have every right to feel that way. But letting it chew away at you will force you to push everyone away."

I sighed. "Sounds like you have experience."

Maverick hummed and nodded his head. "Yeah. Remember Alexis?" I shook my head. "Well turned out she was fucking just about every man behind my back. I came home and caught her in bed with some random guy. It crushed me. I was so angry. All I could be grateful for was that I didn't have my gun that day. I probably blown their heads off. For a long time, I vowed I'd never let another person into my life. And I guess I'm still a bit like that. But after a while, I realised I had a choice. I could spend the rest of my life bitter and angry and never let anyone close to me again. Or I could accept that this job is for a single person and live like that."

"I guess that's why most of the relationships that last are the ones that are both cops."

"Yep," Maverick said with a nod. "That's what I thought too. But then I have a rule of no dating another cop."

I chuckled. "You like to make things hard for yourself."

"Na, not really. I figure I'm just not ready for a relationship. I mustn't really want one if I find it easy to not date."

"I understand that. I don't even want to begin to think about dating. Part of me would like to fuck everything that moves just to get under Taylor's skin. You know she's the only person I've ever been with?"

Maverick smiled. "Would that make you feel better?"

I snorted and shook my head. "No. I'm not sure I could get it up for someone else."

"Not now, but you might change your mind later on." Maverick pulled the car into the coroner's office and cut the engine. "Give it time. Focus on you. Learn who you are first."

I smiled and nodded my head. "Derek reckons I should get a lawyer."

Maverick nodded. "I agree. You will have custody to sort out what you want to do with the house. If you want her to have it, either she buys you out or you hand it over. It should all be done through a lawyer."

"I just don't want to make her hate me."

Maverick chuckled. "You know not too many men would be that kind."

I sighed. "I know. I keep thinking about the girls, though. I don't want them to hate me because I mistreated their mum."

"I get that. You're a good man, Harris."

Chapter Thirteen

M averick

"Hey guys," Dean greeted us as we entered his office. I'd already dropped the DNA in for Kelly to start testing. "What have you found out?"

"I'm pretty certain we have a positive match on your John Doe two seventy. I showed the potential victim's brother the tattoo, and he found it Gerard Lopez."

Dean nodded his head and opened the file on his desk that had the images of body parts. "We have two arms, two legs with both feet attached, pelvis and right shoulder. There is no head or torso."

I scrunched my nose. I felt for the family they weren't going to get their whole family member back. Just pieces. Not even enough to even consider having an open coffin. All the body parts would be dumped unceremoniously into a coffin for them to bury.

"You don't think the torso and head could be connected to others?" Harris asked.

"It's possible. I don't have any reports of spare heads, though. All of the John Doe's I sent over were missing heads. Most of their other body parts were accounted for, but every single one was missing their head."

I hummed. "So, maybe he is taking a trophy?"

"Gruesome trophy," Dean groaned.

I nodded my head. But it wasn't unheard of. I had never met a sane killer. Serial killers were the maddest of all. They didn't make any sense to ordinary people. So, it wouldn't have surprised me if the heads were the killer's trophy.

"I've dropped in DNA to Kelly for Gerard. Once that is confirmed, we can release the body."

"Good, they have been here too long. He deserves a proper burial."

I nodded my head. "I agree. What can you tell me about the death?"

Dean looked down at his file. "Because of the state of decomposition, it was hard to tell the actual cause. It was obviously homicide, but what actually killed him, I can't tell you. Especially with the missing body parts."

My shoulders dropped with deflation. That made our job harder. If we didn't know how these guys died, then it could take even longer to find the killer. "There was no trauma to the body parts that you have?" Harris asked.

"Nothing other than being cut up, which happened after death."

"What with?"

"Chainsaw, I believe."

"Jesus, which would have made some messy work."

Dean nodded his head. "Yep. I don't believe that it was done at the dump site. No pools of blood were found in the area. I believe that our John Doe had been dead about a week by the time the body parts were found. While I can account for animal activity or rain, this wasn't the case. I'd noted that we hadn't had any rain in two weeks, and the animals wouldn't lick the blood off the ground. They are more likely to only eat the meat."

I hummed. "I wonder if animals dragged the head and torso away?"

Dean shrugged his shoulders. "It's possible. We searched the area but couldn't find any other parts. The only animals that are likely to be able to carry a torso away are foxes or maybe stray dogs. However, they unlikely have carried them away and left the small body parts."

"That's true. It might be worth us going and looking at the dump site anyway. Especially now that we have a potential name and track to follow," I said as I glanced over at Harris, who nodded.

"Yeah, I think that's a good idea."

I tapped my hand on the desk in front of me and stood. "Alright, thanks, man; Xavier will drop in other DNA samples for a match on other bodies. But I will no doubt be back in touch soon."

Dean smiled and waved his hands. "It's always a pleasure, gentlemen."

I chuckled and waved as Harris and I left the office. First, I wanted to go to the Pink Flamingo to speak with the owner, Lincoln Master and bartender Tyler. Then we would go and check out at least the dump site where Gerard's body was left. All I hoped was that we would be able to bring this killer to justice sooner than later. I hated the fact that there was someone targeting men, but knowing that they were targeting my community of men made me want blood even more.

Chapter Fourteen

Xavier

"Thank you for meeting with me, Mr and Mrs Lewis. I'm sorry we are meeting under these circumstances," I said as I shook Mr Lewis's hand.

"Please call us Stephen and Vanessa," Stephen said. I sat on the chair opposite them in the interview room and placed the folder containing the missing person's report about their son Koby.

"I wanted to speak to you about Koby's disappearance," I explained.

Vanessa's brows pinched, and exchanged a glance with her husband. "You said that you are from the homicide unit. Does that mean Koby was murdered?" she asked. Vanessa's voice quivered with emotion.

I licked over my bottom lip as I tried to think about how I would approach this conversation. It was challenging, and I couldn't predict how they would react.

"That is what I want to discuss with you. In the missing person's report, you noted that Koby had a large scar along his bicep and a tattoo on one of his hips." Stephen and Vanessa nodded their heads. "This might be distressing to see, but I'm wondering if you would mind looking at a photo to see if you can identify both the scar and tattoo?"

My nerves had ramped up as I prepared to show Koby's parents pictures of his body that had been cut up and discarded like he was rubbish.

"Yes," Stephen answered, but I could see there was no way he was prepared for what he was about to see.

"Before I show you, I must warn you that these photos aren't nice."

"It's okay," Stephen said. He looked like he was only just hanging on while Vanessa was openly crying, and her face was pale.

With a nod, I opened the folder and slipped out the two photos I'd prepared to see them. A groan fell from Vanessa's lips, and she turned away. "I'm going to be sick."

I quickly leapt from the chair and stuck the rubbish bin beneath her just as she vomited. I stroked my hand over her back as she purged everything in her stomach, and the retching turned into sobs.

I took the tissues from the table and placed them in her hand. She glanced up and nodded her head in thanks. I went to the interview room door and stuck my head out.

"Hey, Jess?" I called the cop, who was seated at the nearest desk. She looked up at me and smiled. "Could you please get a bottle of water?"

"Of course," she replied, smiling, standing from her desk before entering the kitchen.

I returned to the desk and sat back down. Vanessa had her head in her hands as she leaned over the bin. Her shoulders shook with cries. Stephen continued to stare at the photo. Slowly, he reached out and traced his fingers over the scar that ran down the victim's arm.

"Stephen, is that Koby?" I asked quietly.

His jaw tightened, and he nodded a small head. Stephen cleared his throat and looked up at me with red eyes that were filled with tears. "Yes. That's Koby."

I swallowed and nodded as Jess opened the door with two water bottles. I smiled over at her. "Thank you, Jess."

"No problems. Do you want me to take this from you?" Jess asked Vanessa as she pointed to the bin.

Vanessa nodded her head. "Yes. I don't think I have anything left."

"Okay," Jess replied as she picked up the bin and left the interview room.

"Take a sip of water," I instructed as I pushed the bottle toward Vanessa.

Once she turned and took the bottle, I quickly put the pictures away in the folder again.

"I am so sorry," I said with a shake. "I wish there was a mistake in this, and it was all nothing more than a coincidence." Stephen and Vanessa said nothing, but both nodded. "The only other thing I'd like to do is do a DNA swab on you both just to make sure that this body definitely belongs to Koby."

Stephen nodded again. "Of course."

"What happened to him?" Vanessa cried.

"At the moment, I can't answer that. We are trying to get those answers for you."

Vanessa sighed and folded her arms across her chest, hugging herself tight. "Can I take my baby home?"

"You will be able to, yes. The coroner's office will give you a call when you can move his body to the funeral home."

"Thank you," she said quietly. "It all feels like a nightmare."

"I understand that. And once again, I'm so sorry that I've had to come to you with this news. I'll go and organise to get the DNA swabs done, then you will be free to go home."

I stood from the chair and walked out of the office to find Riley, who had administered the DNA swabs.

Chapter Fifteen

Harris

We pulled into the carpark at the Pink Flamingo. "Have you ever been here before?" Maverick asked with a knowing grin.

I rolled my eyes and chuckled. "No."

"It's camp."

I threw my head back and laughed. "I wouldn't expect anything less."

Maverick laughed and climbed from the car. I followed him into the club and looked around. He wasn't lying. Every wall was a hot pink with purple accents. There were large painted portraits of naked men that lined the walls in gold frames. I followed Maverick down a long hallway leading to a row of offices.

Maverick knocked on one of the doors, and I heard someone call out. He swung the door open, and we walked into the most exquisite office space I'd ever seen. The walls were walnut, and an enormous ebony desk sat in the middle.

"Mav, Tyler said you'd be calling in. How's it going?" the man said. If I was a gay man, I would have rolled my tongue back up in my head. Even I could see how attractive he was.

"Linc, this is my partner, Harris," Maverick said with a smile.

Lincoln looked over at me and gave me a smile. "Nice to meet you. Have a seat, guys and tell me what I can do for you. I'm assuming that it is business and not personal?"

I sat in an oversized leather chair beside Maverick, who smiled and nodded. "Yeah. We've been made aware of eighteen men who have gone missing, and the last place they were known to be was here. I have confirmation of at least one that has been found murdered."

"Shit," Lincoln groaned. "Someone is targeting here?"

Maverick nodded his head. "That's what I'm starting to think. I don't have complete confirmation until we get the DNA results back, matching the other bodies to the missing men. But I've got a feeling that we are dealing with a serial killer."

Lincoln leaned back in his seat and sighed. "What do I need to do?"

Maverick breathed in deeply and let it out. "To be honest, I don't know. I'm at a bit of a loss on this one. We don't even have any possible suspects for it."

"Could it be a coincidence that the guys were here before they went missing?"

"If it were just one or two guys, I would agree. But not eighteen," I said.

Lincoln nodded his head. "Yeah, you've got a point."

"Have you happened to notice any weird guys hanging about?" I questioned.

Lincoln frowned and folded his arms across his chest as he shook his head. "Not that I know of. Tyler would definitely be the one to ask about that. Can you tell me some of the names? Maybe I can help more with that?"

Maverick nodded and scanned through his phone. "The first victim that we have confirmation of is Gerard Lopez."

Lincoln frowned and shook his head. "I don't know him. What are the others?"

Maverick listed the names that we had marked as missing. Lincoln listened and shook his head to each name until he reached Kai Green. "Wait, Kai, yeah, I know Kai. He used to work here. He was one of my bartenders, but he had just stopped coming to work, and I couldn't contact him. I had no idea he was reported missing. Who reported him?"

Maverick looked down at his phone again as he scanned Kai's file. "His grandmother, Sheryl."

"I didn't realise he had family. He told me that he was on his own."

I hummed. I wondered if Kai was lying about his work or perhaps his grandmother was the only one he had, and he wasn't close to her.

"Did you notice Kai getting close to anyone on his last shift?" I asked.

Lincoln shook his head. He lifted his phone from his desk and pressed on the screen before bringing it up to his ear. "Hey Tyler, can you come to my office please?"

He ended the call and placed his phone back on the table. "If he was getting close to anyone, Tyler would know. They were working together."

I glanced over at Maverick, who frowned. "Tyler doesn't fraternise with customers," he mused.

"Yeah, that's right."

"What about with co-workers?" I asked.

Lincoln's eyes widened, and he gasped before shaking his head. "No. Tyler most definitely isn't the guy you're looking for. I trust him with my life. He would never do something like this."

I nodded. I couldn't tell because I didn't know Tyler. Before I could say anything more, the office door opened, and a handsome young guy entered. "Hey, Mav," he greeted. Everyone knew my damned partner.

"Hey, Tyler," he answered before explaining why we were there. Tyler listened with wide eyes. "One of the missing men is Kai Green."

Tyler's mouth dropped open, and he gasped. "Oh shit, you mean he was possibly killed?"

Maverick nodded his head. "Yeah, we need to confirm it first. Actually, you might be able to help. If I show you a picture of a ring that the body believes Kai's, would you recognise it?"

Tyler nodded his head. "Yeah, he always wore a ring."

Maverick scrolled on his phone and returned the photo before turning it in for Tyler.

"Yeah, that's his," he said with a sad shake.

Maverick nodded. "Thank you. On that night, did you see anyone Kai went home with?"

Tyler hummed, and he scratched at the back of his neck. "I feel like there was a guy he was talking to at the bar, but we were pretty busy. I remember thinking I wanted Kai to stop flirting with the patron and do his job."

"Can you describe the guy?"

Tyler shook his head. "No. I didn't really take any notice of him. I see so many faces that they don't even really stick in my mind anymore."

"What about any of the other guys?" I asked. "Have you noticed them talking, drinking or dancing with anyone?"

Tyler hummed. "I'm sorry. I really don't know."

"Tyler, I'm not saying you're a person of interest, but I have to ask, where were you on the night Kai went missing?"

Tyler's eyes widened slightly before he schooled his face. "I was here until four, and then I went home."

"Is there anyone that can alibi you?"

Tyler frowned and shook his head. "Lincoln was here when I left, but I live alone."

"Was Kai already gone by the time you left?" I asked.

Tyler nodded his head. "Yeah, he finished his shift at two."

I glanced at Lincoln, who nodded his head. "How come you stay so late?"

"That night, there was a huge cleanup. We'd had a party in, and they destroyed the place. Usually, I leave at three."

I nodded. That made sense. "Alright, thank you," Maverick said. "Can you take extra notice of the patrons over the next few weeks? Anyone who might look like they are creeping or just out of place may be a bit pushier to get the guys out of the club. Can you let me know? Also, if we can get any footage available for Saturday night? Our last missing guy was here then."

"Yeah, of course," Lincoln answered. "I'll email you the footage to you."

"Thanks, Linc," Maverick answered before he slid a card out of his pocket and handed it to Lincoln. "I'm going to be more present here until we find out what the hell is happening."

"Thank you. I appreciate you doing that. I hate the idea that someone is killing these kids."

"Me too," Mav answered before he stood, and I followed him out of the office. "Let's go and visit a few of the dump sites."

I nodded and followed Maverick out of the club to the car. It was time to find this guy. Eighteen kids were too many. This killer needed to be ended sooner rather than later.

Chapter Sixteen

Killer

    I'd been getting brazen with my kills, and I knew it would catch up if I wasn't more careful. I stood against the wall of the Pink Flamingo. The place was crawling with cops. They thought they were slick and hiding but stuck out like sore thumbs. Especially the straight cops that were comfortable being surrounded by the faggots in their mesh shirts and their asses hanging out.

I watched the main cop who visited here often, Maverick. He sat at the bar sipping on his beer. He wasn't here for pleasure. I could tell by how he sipped on the beer rather than drinking like usual. He didn't even know that I was watching him. He was utterly oblivious to me. He always had been. But I was aware of him.

I turned my attention to the guy that sat next to him. He looked like he wanted to be anywhere other than at the bar. Bags were under his eyes, and he continued yawning like he was out way after bedtime. A young guy walked toward Maverick and gave him a smile.

Maverick winked and reached out, pulling the guy between his widened legs. The guy sitting beside Maverick turned his head so as not to notice the flirting. I felt my stomach roll in disgust as Maverick leaned in and kissed the guy. The guy was lapping it up completely.

I scoffed and shook my head. They all flocked to Maverick like he was some kind of god. He never went home without someone. He was a slut. It made me sick. My lip curled over my top teeth, and I turned my head.

"An ex?" a voice called from beside me.

I startled slightly and turned to face the guy. Another fucking cop. I'd seen this one here occasionally but didn't know his name.

"Yeah," I replied. It wasn't true. I had no idea who the guy was with Maverick, but I had to cover my ass.

"Which one?"

I pointed with my head. "The twink getting it on with the cop."

"Oh, you know the cop?"

I snorted, nodded, and looked the guy up and down. "You all kind of stand out. What are you all doing here?"

The cop beside me frowned but then cocked his head to the side. "Have you heard about men going missing?"

I raised my brows and feigned shock. "No. From here?"

The cop nodded his head. He pulled his phone out of his pocket and scrolled on the screen. "Do you know this?"

The cop turned his phone to face me, and I saw my last victim. He was smiling at the camera, standing with a woman that could have been his mother. I shook my head.

"I might've seen him here before, but I can't be sure."

The cop searched my face for a moment before he nodded his head. He moved his thumb over his phone screen and returned it to me. "What about him?"

I had to fight with everything inside me as I looked at the first fucker I'd killed. I nodded my head. "Yeah, I remember him," I said as I pointed at the screen. "He hasn't been in for ages. But I remember him because he danced on the stage regularly."

The cop nodded and put his phone back in his pocket before pulling out a business card and handing it to me. "I'm Detective Xavier Cooper. Did you notice Gerard leaving with anyone the last time he was here?"

I tapped on my chin with Xavier's card and hummed. "I can't say for sure. It's been ages since I've seen him. But most of the guys go home with someone."

Xavier nodded. "What is your name?"

"Santo," I answered. It fell from my lips before I had a chance to stop it. Usually, I never gave my real name. I wasn't sure why I did it now.

Xavier smiled and grinned in return. From the look on his face, he had no idea that he was standing right in front of the reason that all of these men were dead.

"Thanks, Santo. If you have any information or know of other guys that seem to have disappeared, can you give me a ring?"

"Sure," I answered, waving his card and placing it in my pocket.

Xavier smiled again and walked away. I watched him and scanned the room. Maverick was still focused on his pickup, but the cop that had been sitting beside Maverick now watched me with narrowed eyes. I lifted my hand in a wave. He frowned but looked away, making me chuckle. I lifted my bottle to my mouth and sucked down the rest of it. There was going to be no killing tonight. It would be too dangerous. I reached into my pocket and pulled out my keys. It was going to be an early night tonight.

Chapter Seventeen

Maverick

"I can't tonight, Joachin," I said to the cute twink pressed against my body. "I'm working."

Joachin's eyes widened, and he gasped. "You're working here?"

I nodded my head. "Have you noticed guys going missing from here?"

Joachin frowned and shrugged. "Maybe a few. I mean, I just assumed they had boyfriends or something. I didn't think that it was anything criminal."

I squeezed his hips. "Yeah, it is."

"Wait, you're a homicide cop. Does that mean they are being murdered?"

I sighed and nodded my head.

"Shit," Joachin spat. "Is it someone targeting this particular club?"

"I don't know, but that's why I'm here. Have you noticed any weirdos or heard from others about creepers?"

Joachin chuckled. "There are loads of fucking creepers that hang around here."

"Yeah?" I said with a raised brow.

"Of course there is. They prey on places like this, hoping to find some young guy just stepping out of the closet."

I sighed as I realised he was telling the truth. Plenty of guys were always prepared to take advantage of a young person. It made me angry, but technically, they weren't doing anything illegal, so there wasn't anything I could do.

"Do you know any of their names?"

Joachin nodded his head. "Yeah, I can write them down and ask some other guys, too?"

"Yeah, that would be good," I said as I leaned forward and pressed my lips against his. "Just be careful. Don't go home with people you don't know."

"You mean like you?"

I threw my head back and laughed and nodded. "Yeah, like me."

Joachin pouted his plump bottom lip and looked at me with big eyes. "But I had so much fun."

I felt my cock stir in my pants and growled in my throat. "Another day, minx."

Joachin giggled and moved away from my body. He wiggled his fingers in a wave and walked into the throng of people. I glanced over at Harris, who was glaring around at the crowd. I knew he didn't want to be here.

"Anything stands out?" I asked.

Harris sighed and shook his head. "No. Xavier was talking to a guy, but he was just left alone. I don't think there was anything in it."

Xavier came and stood beside me. Soon, Nathan and Landyn joined us. "I've spoken to a few regular guys," Xavier said. "I've asked them to spread the word that guys are being targeted and to let us know if they see anything suspicious."

I nodded my head. "Yeah, I've spoken to some regulars too."

Xavier nodded. "I don't know that anything is going to happen tonight. The last guy that I spoke to, a Santo, he picked us as cops. If he did, I suspect anyone else might, too."

I chuckled and nodded. "I have no doubt, but hopefully, that might be enough to make him a little wary about killing anyone."

"Hopefully, he won't move to a different club," Landyn commented.

That was a risk we had to take. We'd looked at all the missing person reports, and so far, none of the others had been missing from other clubs. Just this one. It was something we were going to have to keep an eye on. We were chasing our tails and didn't know who our killer was. Until we had some more direction, we floated in the wind. It was frustrating. I looked around the dance floor. For all I knew, our killer was here watching us, and we had no idea.

"Come on, let's get going. We've got to some crime scenes to go and visit; hopefully, something might come up," I directed.

We all left, I waved at Tyler as I passed the bar. It felt like it was a waste of a night, but at the same time, if we had been able to make the guys aware that someone was targeting them, it might not have been a waste after all.

Chapter Eighteen

Harris

"Morning," I grumbled as I stared into my coffee, and Maverick moved into the kitchen. Thor let out a long yowl. I was sure the cat was dobbing on me for not giving him food.

"Have you slept at all?" Maverick asked as he picked up Thor's food bowl and rinsed it in the sink before drying it and filling it with food.

I sighed and shrugged my shoulders. "I got a few hours."

Maverick hummed and placed the cat's bowl on the floor. Thor leapt from the bench and went to his bowl to eat. "That's not enough."

I shrugged again. "I can't force my body to sleep."

Maverick sat down beside me. "I know. If it continues, you might need to see the doctor?"

I nodded. I didn't want to. But Maverick was right. Not sleeping would affect my job, and I didn't want that to happen. My career and kids were all I had left to keep me sane.

"Have you heard from Taylor?"

I shook my head. "I haven't turned my phone back on."

Maverick frowned and nodded. "You're going to have to speak to her at some stage. You've got to sort out at least visitation with the kids."

I sighed and rubbed my hands over my face. "It all feels too much. Whenever I think about turning my phone back on to speak to her or ring a law firm, it gets too much, and I can't do it." Admitting my weakness was killing me. But I had to admit to myself and Maverick that I couldn't keep going. I was breaking inside. I didn't know how to end a relationship. Taylor had been the only person I'd ever been with.

"Alright, I'm going to make a list," Maverick said as he stood from the table and rummaged through one of the drawers to pull out a notepad and pen. He came, sat back down, and tapped the pen on the paper before writing. "Right, so first, you must sort out a lawyer and child support. It's Saturday, so there is no point in ringing them today, but that will be the first thing you must do on Monday. Once those two steps are done, you can think more about whether you will sell the house and stuff next."

I shook my head. "I don't want to sell the house. I will walk away from it."

Maverick frowned. "That's honourable of you to do. But you are going to need money to get yourself a place. I mean, you can stay here as long as you want. I have no issue with that. But you're going to eventually want some of your independence back."

Living alone was probably the one thing that terrified me more than anything. But Maverick was right. I couldn't stay here forever. He needed his own space. And I needed to learn how to live without someone.

"Okay, I'll be able to face that."

Maverick smiled at me. "First, let's give Taylor a ring. I think the two of you need to talk about what the two of you expect moving forward. Regardless of your marriage breakdown, you've got the girls to think about, and you have to co-parent."

I sighed and buried my face in my hands. I groaned.

"I know. I know," Maverick chuckled. "I'll come with you. Now go and turn your phone on, and I'll make breakfast, and then we will call her and sort something out."

I groaned but stood from the kitchen table and moved back into the bedroom that I was using. I had turned my phone off the minute I'd left the house a week earlier. The thought of speaking to Taylor made my stomach turn sour. I loved my girls with everything in me, and if it weren't for them, I wouldn't talk to Taylor again. But once again, Maverick was right. Fuck him for being right all the damned time.

Once my phone booted, a series of beeps sounded from missed calls and messages. I looked at the screen and saw that Taylor had tried to ring me and left many messages. I cleared them without listening to them. I couldn't do it. I scrolled through the other messages. There was a couple from my parents. I ran my hand down over my face. I had to break the news to my parents. They probably already knew because I had no doubt that Taylor would have told them.

I pressed Mum's number and put the phone to my ear. "Harris, thank god," she answered.

"Hey, Mum," I replied. My voice quivered under the weight of sadness on my shoulders.

"Oh, Harry, sweetheart. I'm sorry."

I sighed and nodded. "I don't know what I did wrong."

"Nothing. You did nothing wrong, sweetheart. Taylor's choices were her choices to make. She could have come to you if she wasn't happy."

"That's what I don't understand. Why didn't she come to me? I would have quit my job if that was what she wanted. I would have done everything to make her happy."

"I know you would have. Where are you?"

"I'm at Mavericks."

"Good, I'm glad. Are you working on a case at the moment?"

"Yeah. I'm glad I am. It is keeping me busy."

"Don't let it consume, though, Harris. Those girls still need you. It would be hard not to pour yourself into work and ignore everything else."

"Yeah. I'm going to speak to Taylor today so that I can work something out for the girls."

"Good. Listen, sweetheart, I want you to come home one night and have dinner with us. Bring Maverick, too."

I smiled and felt a little bit lighter after speaking with Mum. "I will. Thank you."

"Anytime. I love you."

"I love you too," I said before ending the call. It was silly. I should have spoken to my mother a week ago. I felt a lot better after talking to her. I needed it.

Chapter Nineteen

Maverick

"You ready?" I asked Harris as we pulled into the house's driveway, which he shared with Taylor.

Harris sighed and nodded his head. Suddenly, the front door opened, and two little girls came dashing down the front stairs to the driveway.

"Daddy," Daisy squealed with excitement.

"Do it for them," I murmured as Harris swung the passenger door open and stepped out. He wiped the sadness off his face and grinned at Daisy as he swept her into his arms and kissed her cheek.

Imogen stood at the bottom of the stairs, watching warily. I could tell from the look in her eye that she knew more than they realised. I walked to the steps and lifted her into my arms.

"You, okay?" I asked.

Imogen looked into my eyes. Her face crumpled as she shook her head. I pulled her tight against me as her little body started to shake with tears. "It will be alright, little one," I soothed, stroking my hand along her back. It was tearing at my heart to see her like this. Harris looked up at me and frowned.

He walked toward me and reached out his arms. Awkwardly, Imogen and Daisy traded spaces, and Imogen clung to her father as her sobs became louder.

"Mum told us that she and Daddy weren't going to live together anymore," Daisy said quietly.

I nodded my head. "I know. How do you feel about that?"

She shrugged her shoulders. "We will still see Daddy?"

I nodded again. "Definitely. I wouldn't have it any other way."

"Then it will be okay, I guess. I will miss not seeing him every day."

"I'm sure he will miss that too. But that doesn't change how much he loves you."

Daisy smiled and nodded her head. For all that little girl had been through, the one thing she'd never lost was her hair and her faith in Harris. He was the star in her eyes. Slowly, we entered the house where Taylor was sitting at the table. She glanced up as we walked in but didn't say anything. She turned her attention back to the coffee that I suspected was cold.

"Let's go outside and talk," Harris told the girls.

Imogen clung to his neck and refused to be put down as he walked toward the back door. I watched out the dining room window as he led them to their cubby house at the rear of the yard and climbed awkwardly inside. That little cubby house had many happy memories for Harris and the girls. So often, I would come to the house, and he'd be out there with the girls having a tea party. He was a fantastic father. Despite his long hours, he still ensured his girls knew how much they were loved. This was going to screw with all of their heads.

I walked over to the table and sat down opposite Taylor. She looked up and gave me a tight smile. "Do you think I'm a monster for this?"

I shook my head. "No. I think you've mishandled it. I won't ever understand why you chose to cheat instead of coming to Harris first, but I don't think you're a monster."

Taylor sighed, and tears welled in her eyes. "I never intended to cheat."

"Taylor, no one accidentally cheats."

She nodded her head and then shrugged her shoulders. "I know. I know it was a purposeful choice, but it didn't feel like that then."

"How did it start?" I asked.

Taylor looked up at me and frowned. "When Daisy's cancer came back. Jason came over one day when Harris was at the hospital. I was sobbing because I thought we were going to lose her. She was sick, and I didn't think she would beat it this time. Jason was here, and he hugged me. I don't know how or who started it, but he hugged me one minute, and we were making out and everything the next minute."

I frowned and leaned back in the seat. "Why didn't you put a stop to it then?"

Taylor shrugged. "I don't know. I can't explain it."

"Didn't you feel wanted by Harris?"

Taylor laughed humourlessly. "I always felt wanted by Harris. I don't think it was ever about the physical act of sex. Jason took something away from me that Harris didn't. I was able to pretend that everything was alright in my world. None of the fear I felt around Daisy existed when we were together."

"And now?"

"And now, I've fallen in love with him."

I nodded my head. It hurts to think how easily someone's emotions could change. I hurt for Harris and the girls. "You know that there are going to be a lot of changes now?"

Taylor nodded. "Yeah. We need to sort out custody and the house. Is he going to fight for custody?"

I snorted and rolled my eyes. "Taylor, you know that man better than anyone else. You know that he won't fight you for anything. All I ask is you let him walk away and be good to him in this."

Taylor's brows pulled into a frown. "I don't want to fight him."

I nodded. "Good. He deserves that much."

Chapter Twenty

Harris

I wanted to completely crumble when I looked into Imogen's eyes. Her heart was breaking, and it was destroying me. But there was nothing I could do. I couldn't change what had happened and what was about to happen. This had been all Taylor's making. I wanted to be angry. God, I wanted to hate her, and I guess somewhere deep inside, I probably did, and I knew that the anger and bitterness would emerge, and that would be a whole new slew of things I would have to overcome.

"Daddy, are you going to be living with Uncle Mav?" Daisy asked as we sat on the edge of the cubby house.

I nodded my head. "For a little while. Until I get a house of my own."

Imogen shook her head. "I don't want you to leave. I want you to stay here," she sobbed.

I sighed. I didn't know how I was going to handle this. "I know, sweetheart. Listen, sometimes Mummies and Daddies just don't work together anymore. So, instead of always fighting, they need to get away from each other, which means they don't live together anymore."

"But you and Mum never fight," Imogen growled.

This little girl was far more observant and wiser than we'd given her credit for. "We don't have to fight out loud to have problems. Have you ever met someone, and after all, you realise you don't want to be their friend anymore?"

Imogen sighed and shrugged her shoulders. "Not really. Is it because of Jason?"

My eyes widened, and I had to school my face quickly. "What about Jason?" I asked.

Imogen's lip curled over her top teeth in a snarl. "He was kissing Mum."

I felt repulsion was over me. It was one thing to know that they had been fucking, but to understand that the girls had seen them together.

I breathed in deeply as I tried to check my words. "Mum and Jason have fallen in love with each other."

"I hate him," Imogen growled.

Daisy nodded her head. "Me too."

I winced. I wanted to feel bad for Taylor, but she'd made her bed. The girls weren't going to have any respect for Jason. Not that he deserved any. I didn't know what to say. I'd always taught my girls to show adults respect and behave, but I didn't have it in me to do the same here. Jason didn't deserve their respect. Instead of being a fucking man and coming to me and sharing what was going on, he'd been absent.

"Can I live with you when you get a house?" Imogen asked, drawing me out of my thoughts.

I blinked and frowned. "We will talk about that later on. At the moment, I'm staying with Uncle Mav, and then I'll have to find somewhere to live that fit you girls in as well."

"I don't want to stay with Mum," Imogen insisted.

I smiled and ran my hand down over her hair. "I know that you are angry at the moment. But your Mum still loves you very much, and you must be a good girl."

Imogen folded her arms across her chest. "Why? If she didn't kiss Jason, you and she wouldn't be breaking up, and we could have our Dad living here. I don't want to live with her and Jason."

My brows furrowed, and I cocked my head to the side. "I don't think you will be living with Jason."

Daisy nodded her head. "Yes, we will. Mummy and Jason told us that last night. Mummy wants us to move into his house."

I groaned and scrubbed my hand down over my face. That was too much. If it wasn't enough that she was cheating on me, now she was demanding that our daughters will be moving in with her and him. He was planning on taking over my role.

"I will talk to Mum," I said quietly. I didn't know what to do. Anything more I had to say wasn't going to be polite.

Thankfully, I heard the back door open and saw Maverick approaching us. "I'm going to talk to Mum. You girls stay out here with Uncle Mav."

Imogen nodded and moved from my lap beside her sister as I stood. "Everything alright?" he asked.

I shook my head. "They know about Jason. She told them that they would be moving in with him."

"Christ," Maverick spat. "Go and speak to her. Stay as calm as possible."

I nodded my head. I didn't know how that was going to be possible. I wanted to destroy everything. I walked into the house and saw Taylor sitting at the dining table. She glanced up at me and tried to smile. I couldn't muster the same courtesy.

"Do you hate me?" she asked.

I sighed and sat down opposite her. "No. I think there will come a time when I will. But right now, no."

Taylor's eyes welled with tears, and she shook her head. "I didn't mean for it to happen."

I scoffed and shook my head. "Yes, I've often had problems where I accidentally lost all of my clothes and fucked someone."

She sighed. "Harris, it wasn't like that. It wasn't some nefarious act."

"Then what was it, Taylor? You fucked someone else. You destroyed our marriage."

Taylor scoffed and shook her head. "Harris, this marriage was destroyed before I did anything with Jason."

I raised my brow. Was it? How did I miss that? "How?"

"I was unhappy, Harris. Daisy's cancer took so much from me. Add your job and the number of times you weren't home. It was enough to break us."

I frowned. "I knew you were unhappy, but I thought that was because of Daisy's cancer. I thought you were unhappy because you were afraid that she was going to die."

"I was."

"But how did that turn into being our marriage not working?"

"I don't know, Harris. I don't know. I can't explain it because you don't want to believe me when I say I never meant it to happen."

I scrubbed my hands over my face. "The girls told me you plan on moving in with Jason."

Taylor looked down at the table, her cheeks tinted pink, and she nodded. "Maverick said you would walk away, but I don't want to live here anymore."

"How long had you been planning to move in with Jason?" I growled.

She looked up at me with wide eyes as she shook her head. "Why does that matter?"

"Because I'm trying to see how much of an accident your affair was. Was it a mistake if you've planned to move in with him since the beginning?"

"Harris, look, I'm sorry. I don't know what else I can say. I get you are angry, and you have every right to be angry. But what do you want from me?"

I chuckled, but my laugh had no humour, so I shook my head. "I want nothing from you, Taylor. Absolutely fucking nothing. We will organise the selling of the house and halve the assets. Do we need to go to court to visit the girls? Will Jason be okay that I father my children?"

Taylor's eyes widened, and she gasped. "I don't want you to be like this."

"You don't get to control how I am. You don't get to control my anger, my emotions, my feelings. You don't control that. So, do I have to go to family court or not?"

Taylor shook her head. "No. You can have the girls as often as you like."

I nodded my head. "I will take them every weekend then."

Taylor nodded but stayed silent. I stood from the table and looked down at her. Disgust filled me. This wasn't the woman I'd fallen in love with. This wasn't the girl who stole my heart.

"I'll have my lawyer contact you about everything else," I said before turning and walking doubt of the door toward the girls. I gave them kisses and cuddles and promised I would be there next weekend to take them to Mav's house. Neither wanted me to leave, but I couldn't stay there anymore. The thought of being close to Taylor was sickening. I couldn't do it. And I hated feeling that way.

Chapter Twenty-One

Xavier

I looked around the bridge, where there were body parts strewn below. "I've got everything except the head," Kelly said from beside.

"Same as the other ones?"

Kelly shrugged her shoulders. "Possibly, we won't know until we have a DNA match."

I sighed. "This is frustrating."

Kelly nodded her head. "I will compare anything with the other bodies, but from what I can tell from the reports, none of the other bodies had any DNA left on them."

I nodded. "Yeah, and with them being found a while ago, there is a good chance that there would be no evidence at the scene."

"Looking around, I see that there isn't much here either. This man wasn't killed and dismembered here. This was just a dump site."

"That's what makes it even more frustrating. Our killer is so fucking clean. I don't understand how he is doing it."

Kelly hummed and nodded her head. I'd been reading over every man's missing report and the found body reports, and there was nothing that stood out. The only thing that even linked the guys was the Pink Flamingo. But that wasn't enough.

"Have you looked at the video footage of the night that your last victim went missing?"

I nodded. "It rewrites every twenty-four hours, so the footage wasn't available."

Kelly frowned. "Who the hell still uses tapes anymore?"

I shrugged. "Yeah, I wondered that too. Then it made me wonder if we could make anything out even if the videos were available."

"That's true. Good chance they would still be on disc or worse, VHS."

I snorted and nodded. "Yeah. Just to make our lives a little more difficult," I said as I held my fingers up.

Kelly chuckled. She clasped my shoulder and gave it a squeeze. "If anyone can solve this mess, it's you guys. I believe that."

"Thanks, Kelly. You have more faith in us than I do right now."

She winked and walked away, and I was joined by Harris and Maverick. "Sure, seems connected. Are we thinking it is Michel's body?" Harris asked.

"Yeah. Kelly said all the body parts except the head are there. From the reports, only Gerard was missing more than his head."

"Which could have been possible animal activity," Maverick said.

I nodded my head. "I'm leaning toward that. All of the other bodies have only been missing their heads."

"I wonder what he is doing with them," Harris shuddered.

"It has to be some kind of sick trophy," Maverick mused.

I nodded again. Most serial killers tended to keep some kind of trophy. I'd not come against anyone who kept the heads of their victims, but nothing surprised me anymore.

"Have forensics scoured the rest of the area?" Harris asked.

"Yeah, and there is nothing. The other sites would be the same, but it might be worth checking them. They were the first victims, particularly Gerard's and Rabin's."

Maverick nodded. "I agree. Harris and I will go out there now. Do you want to wrap up here?"

I smiled and gave him a thumbs-up as they turned and walked away. I stared up at the bridge. We'd gone over it, and there was nothing of note. It was an asphalted road, which meant no tyre tracks or anything that might give us a bit of a heads-up. The bridge was in the middle of nowhere, so it wasn't like there would even be a doorbell camera to get some footage. I scrubbed my hand over my face. I had no idea what we were looking for. I needed him to make a mistake. All I could hope was that he fucked up in the beginning, and Maverick or Harris found something. Otherwise, I worried about how many others would die before we found him.

Chapter Twenty-Two

Maverick

I pulled the car to the side of the road and hummed. "A bridge. Could this be a common theme, too?" I pondered.

Harris pulled out his phone, and the files were in front of us. His fingers moved over the screen as he typed in the addresses of the dump sites. "Yep. All bridges."

I hummed again. "I wonder if they form a pattern, which would be really helpful because we might be able to predict where his next dump site would be?"

Harris shook his head. "No, there doesn't appear to be any pattern to it. The only thing is that they are bridges in the middle of nowhere."

Disappointment hit my chest. "Well, it was hopeful thinking."

"When we return to the office, I want to calculate where the middle ground is about all the bridges. They might be far from the killer's house or the Pink Flamingo. It might help us to narrow something down."

I nodded. "It's worth a try. Let's go and have a look and see if we can find something."

Harris swung the passenger door open. I hadn't spoken to him about our visit with Taylor on the weekend. He hadn't said anything to me about it other than that they had agreed to sell the house, and he would take the kids every weekend. I figured if he wanted to know more, he would tell me.

I walked down the embankment to the dry creek bed beneath the bridge. I looked up at the bridge. It was a surprise that anyone found Gerard's body from here.

As if thinking the same thing, Harris interrupted my thoughts. "Who found Gerard's body?"

"A couple of kids riding dirt bikes along the creek bed."

"I wonder if anyone has trail cams along here?"

"It would be helpful if they did." I looked around at the pillars of the bridge. There had been a small amount of vandalism on them, but it was nothing like what I had expected, which said that not many people came to the bridge.

"I can see some tracks up through here," Harris called.

"Animal?"

Harris nodded. "Yeah, probably foxes or deer."

I went to where he stood and started to walk up through the tracks. "If animals did get to Gerard's torso, we may find bones scattered."

"Yeah, that's what I was thinking."

We continued to walk up through the track. The edges were covered with long grass and branches, making it difficult to see much.

"There," Harris said as he stopped and pointed at one of the low-hanging branches of what appeared to be some kind of bracken bush.

I peered closer to see what he was looking at. "Is it material?"

Harris nodded. "It looks like a shirt or something."

I reached into my pocket and pulled out a pair of gloves before handing them over to Harris. He slipped them on his hands and moved his way toward the shirt. Carefully, he untangled the shirt and held it up.

"Is that blood?" I asked, looking at the neck of the shirt.

Harris turned it around and peered close before nodding his head. "Yep. I reckon it is."

I moved in beside Harris and looked further into the bush. There didn't appear to be any other clothes or bones anywhere. Nothing said that it belonged to Gerard, but it might be something.

"We should search this area for any other clothes. It might be that the killer dumps the clothes after the body."

I nodded and started to look around. After a couple of hours searching the entire area, we found a pair of shoes and boxers, all of which appeared to be dried blood coated on them. There were no pants or socks, but it wasn't unusual for us to miss it this long.

"How did Forensics not find this?" I questioned.

Harris shrugged. "What if the killer dumps the clothes once the body has been discovered."

I hummed. "It's possible."

It could happen that way. Especially if the killer wanted to visit the dump site without the chance of being caught. Wait until the body has gone, and then go back. It was a risk that they were taking but not wholly improbable.

Chapter Twenty-Three

Harris

"This is the final dump site," Maverick said as we approached another bridge. "This is where Arpan Kivaraj was found."

I nodded my head. We found clothing with blood on each site we'd visited. After we found what we believed to be Gerard's clothes at the first site, we contacted Kelly to come with us to the other sites so that it could all be documented and collected.

I climbed out of the car and looked over the bridge. "This one has water under it," I commented. It was the first site where there was water under the bridge. All of the others had been dry creek beds or drains.

"This is the one where we found the least body parts. We believed that they floated downstream. The water was a lot higher than this."

"When were the body parts found for this site?" I asked.

"Two and half weeks ago. That seems to be the average time between discoveries, around two and a half weeks."

"And you could definitively match the body parts to Arpan?" Maverick questioned.

Kelly nodded her head. "Yeah. His DNA was already on file. He was why homicide got called in on this case anyway."

I hummed and nodded my head. "How did the other cases not get connected at first?"

Kelly shrugged her shoulders. "I don't know. I think it was because different precincts were working on the cases."

I scratched at my chin. That was the most significant issue we often had. Miscommunication between precincts.

"Did anyone follow the stream to see if they could find other body parts?"

Kelly nodded again. "Yeah, a team of divers travelled about three kilometres downstream. We didn't find anything."

"The water isn't moving that fast. It seems weird that it would have washed them down."

"Yeah, that's what we thought was strange, too. It could be an animal activity, but being close to water will likely attract more animal life."

I hummed. "Let's go and see what we can find."

I moved off the bridge and started climbing to the stream beneath the bridge. It was relatively low, and like Maverick noted, it wasn't running fast, so the reason that more of Arpan's body hadn't been found was strange.

"Why was Arpan's DNA on file?" Maverick asked as we searched through the long reeds on the side of the water.

"He was convicted of rape five years ago. Spent eighteen months in Barwon prison," Kelly answered.

Maverick nodded but didn't say anything. I could tell from the look on his face that he was thinking the same thing. It wasn't a loss. If there was one thing I hated more than anything, it was people who hurt others. Rapists and pedophiles were the lowest form of scum around.

I focused my attention on the bracken that caressed the edges of the stream. Moving slowly, I walked beneath the bridge.

"I've got a body," I said as I suddenly came to a screeching halt. The air around me got dense, and the smell of death hit my nostrils.

"A whole body?" Maverick called.

"Yeah," I replied as I reached for my phone. Maverick and Kelly came to where I was standing and looked down. This wasn't the same as our case. This was a woman; her body was intact, but she had been obviously murdered. Her throat was slashed wide open. Her skin was pale, and her lips twisted in a blue grimace.

"Shit," Maverick spat.

I pressed the phone to my ear and listened to the ring. "Derek Marshall."

"Hey Cap, we've come across a body. Female, throat cut, naked. Possible sexual assault."

"Okay, send me the location, and I'll get Nathan and Brice out there."

I needed the call and sent our location through to Derek. Kelly was on the phone with Dean as Maverick stood looking down at the woman's body.

"What are the fucking chances?" he muttered as he shook his head.

"Yep, now it's going to be hard to tell what is related to her case and Arpan's."

Maverick nodded. "We've probably got enough to work with from the other sites."

It didn't take long before the stream's edge crawled with homicide cops and forensic teams.

"Any idea who she is?" I asked Nathan.

He shook his head sadly. "No. I've got Beau going through the missing person's reports to see if anyone matches her description. From what Kelly said, she hasn't been dead long, maybe twelve or so hours, so she can't have been dumped too long ago. From the scene around her, I would reckon she probably was killed here too."

I frowned. "What the hell would she be doing here?"

Nathan shrugged. "Don't know. There is probably a load of reasons, but judging by her age and the fact that she is naked, I would predict an affair or perhaps a working girl."

"If she's a working girl, she probably won't have anyone report her missing."

Nathan nodded his head and sighed. "Yep. We will know more once Dean gets her back to the coroner's office and starts the autopsy."

"Keep us in the loop," I said, shaking Nathan's hand and leaving. Maverick was in the car waiting when I climbed the embankment toward him.

"What are the fucking odds?"

"You're telling me."

Chapter Twenty-Four

Santo

I glanced around the club floor. The music was much more subdued mid-week than on the weekend. There were new faces. Mostly an after-work crowd. I'd decided to give it a go on a weekday rather than a weekend. It seemed that was when the cops rocked up. I didn't like changing my routine, but if it meant I was successful, that was what I would do.

I'd heard on the television that they found a body at one of the dump sites. As much as I didn't like the idea that someone was using my dump site of their own, it was good. It took the heat off me for a while. I leaned back in the chair and widened my legs as I took a swig of the whiskey that warmed my chest.

Movement caught the corner of my eye, and I glanced at the twink that seemed drawn to Maverick whenever he moved toward me.

"Hi there," he said with a small smile as he slid into the booth beside me.

"Hi, pretty boy," I purred.

His eyes widened slightly, and he licked over his bottom lip in what I assumed was supposed to be seductive. It looked like a dog panting over a bit of meat. Or a head.

My stomach revolted, and anger surged through me. I fought to keep my face neutral as I turned my attention back to the dance floor.

"You don't normally come here on a weekday," he continued.

I turned back to him and nodded my head. "I wanted something different."

"Could I be that difference that you want?"

I leaned forward and looked him up and down. "Maybe. What do you want to do, pretty boy?"

He leaned in and mimicked my stance. "You."

I smirked and nodded my head. I tipped my glass back and swallowed the last whiskey before standing and holding my hand out to the twink. He slipped his fingers into mine and let me lead him out of the club and into the darkened streets.

The bouncer nodded his head. "Be safe, Joachin," he warned as we passed him.

Joachin giggled but didn't pay him any heed. That was going to be his biggest mistake. I continued to lead a giddy Joachin down the back alley to where my car was parked. Opening the back door, I waved my hand for him to climb in. Joachin frowned at me and bit into his bottom lip.

"You are just going to fuck me here?" he asked.

"Where do you want to be fucked?" I questioned, feeling myself getting irritated. I didn't have time for chit-chat. I wanted him to climb in the car to end him and be done with it.

"Well, like a house or a motel. I don't want to just be a quick fuck on the back seat," he pouted.

I rolled my eyes and raised my brow. How did I manage to pick a fucking diva? I couldn't help but think this was my karma for trying to fuck with Maverick.

"Are you too good for a quick fondle in the back seat to warm up?" I growled.

Joachin gasped, and his eyes widened, and I knew that I'd fucked up. "Um. I think I'm going to just go," he said, sounding nervous.

I reached out and snagged his wrist tightly. Joachin gasped and tried to wrench his arm away from me.

"Get in the fucking car," I snarled.

"No," he said, trying to sound harsh, but from the trembling, I knew he wasn't anywhere near as tough as he was trying to portray.

I raised my brow and got in close to his face. "Get in the fucking car," I hissed through clenched teeth.

Tears welled in Joachin's eyes as he shook his head. "Don't. Let me go."

I swung my arm back and curled my fist. With a stiff jab, I slammed my fist into his face and felt his nose crumble under the weight of the punch. Joachin cried out, and his knees buckled. Before I had a chance to grab hold of him again, he let out a blood-curdling scream.

"Shut the fuck up," I roared as I grasped him by the throat and squeezed my hands tight around his neck.

His eyes bulged, and his cheeks bloomed red. Tears streamed and mingled with the blood that dripped from his nose down over his lips and chin. I curled my lip over my top teeth and growled as I slammed him against the side of the car.

"Hey," I heard someone shout. "What the hell are you doing?"

I turned suddenly to see a man running down the alley toward me. My distraction was long enough that Joachin was able to get free. He dashed toward the man who pulled him into his arms.

"Fuck," I spat as I slammed the back door shut and took off down the road and out of the alleyway.

"Get back here," I heard the man call, but I didn't wait. I ran, ducking down alleyways. My heart pounded as I tried to think about my next move. I'd left my car in the alleyway. Fuck. I'd fucked up.

"Fuck," I roared as I came to a stop and pressed my hands into my thighs. I'd fucked up. Fucking Joachin. That fucking little twink was going to make this all go bad.

Chapter Twenty-Five

M averick
"Okay, what can you tell me?" I asked Kelly as I walked into the lab. She looked up and frowned, and shook her head.

"I've been here two hours, Mav. You're being a bit pushy."

I smiled and dropped my head. "I'm sorry," I pouted, making her laugh and roll her eyes.

"Well, lucky for you, I'm just that damned good. I've returned the DNA on three lots of the clothing, and they all match the bodies. I'm still waiting to match some of the DNA of the bodies to make sure they are the missing guys, but I'm pretty much certain they are."

I nodded my head. "Yeah, from the different marks and families we've spoken with, I'd be surprised to see anything different. Were you able to find out about who the girl's body was from yesterday?"

Kelly nodded. "Yeah, a young girl had apparently met a guy on Tinder. Nathan seemed to think that it was him that had killed her."

I shook my head. I hated the concept of dating. Everything was online, and I knew I took just as many risks, but I guess guys didn't necessarily prey on me because I was a big guy. I wasn't someone that was an easy target. All of our victims were small guys with slim builds and twinks. They were the perfect prey to a hunter, just like this girl.

"Hopefully, it's an open and shut case."

Kelly nodded again. "I reckon it will be. He wasn't overly careful about not leaving evidence behind."

"That's good. It will lead to a strong case and an easy conviction."

"Yep. So, how are you going? Getting any closer to finding the guy that handles this?" she asked as she waved her hand over the clothes set out on the benches.

I shook my head. "It's frustrating me. This person has left us with nothing."

"I haven't finished going over the clothes, but there may be some DNA from the killer on them. It is possible he left sweat or something on them. None of the bodies appeared to be sexually assaulted, and there was no evidence of semen, but often, the clothes can tell us more. The downside is that these clothes have been in the elements for a long time. It was a miracle I could get DNA from the blood on them. I don't know if I can get much more."

I smiled and nodded. "Whatever you can give me, Kelly, I appreciate it."

She waved as I left the room and walked toward Dean's office. It had been ages since I'd had a chance for a casual visit with him. They were inseparable since he'd met Carlton, and I didn't see them often. The last I'd heard, they were looking to adopt a child. I rapped my knuckles on the doorframe of the open door and waited for Dean to look up.

He grinned and waved me in. "How's it going?" I asked as I moved into the office and sat beside him.

"I've never had so much damned work. I swear people are dropping like flies out there."

I raised my brows and hummed. "Obviously, not all homicides?"

"There are plenty of them, but no. I'm seeing so many deaths, particularly in younger people, weird causes too, like heart failure, strokes and obscure cancers."

"Yeah? What could it be related to?"

Dean shrugged his shoulders. "I honestly couldn't tell you. If you follow the rabbit hole of conspiracy theorists, you will be told it is all from the Covid vaccination."

"Is there any truth to it?"

"Could be, but really, I don't know. We often don't know the knock-on effects of having the vaccine and then contracting the illness to people. So, I really can't say. But whatever is causing all of these deaths, it's getting worrying. I had a fifteen-year-old boy drop dead on the football oval. He was one minute standing there doing his PE class and the next minute on the ground and dead, couldn't be resuscitated. I opened him up, but his heart was completely blocked. He had a massive heart attack. Looking at the kid, you would never have known he was unhealthy. He was slim, apparently played sports and ate home-cooked meals. A normal kid, yet his cholesterol levels were the same as what you might find in a two hundred kilogram bedridden patient who eats five pizzas a day."

I gasped, and my eyes widened. "Seriously? That is bizarre."

Dean nodded. "Yep, and he isn't the first. Had a guy die after running a marathon, something he did pretty much every weekend. Crossed the finish line and collapsed. By the time the paramedics got him to the hospital, he was dead. Same thing. Completely clogged arteries."

"It doesn't make any sense. I can see why people are blaming the vaccine, though. It's the only new thing to be introduced."

Dean nodded and sighed. "Yeah, that's right. It's just so damned sad. It's hard having to tell the parents of a teenager that their child had the heart of an obese eighty-year-old, and that's what killed him."

I nodded my head. I could only imagine how hard it had been on the parents, and then to have heard the cause of death, I imagined that they would have been in shock and disbelief. I would probably have questioned if the autopsy reports got mixed up if it were me.

"How's everything going with the adoption process?" I asked.

Dean let out a long sigh. "It's not. The girl that we had been going to adopt lost the baby. It was devastating, so we will hold off for a while.

We realised that neither of us is in a position to have a child, so we want to wait."

"I understand that. I'm sorry that happened."

Dean smiled and waved his hand. "Thank you," he said as my phone started to ring. I glanced down at the screen and saw that it was Xavier calling.

"I've got to get this," I said as I stood and walked out of the office, waving my hand to Dean as I left. "Hey Xav, what's up?"

"I've just had a call from Jessie at the front desk. Your twink from the other night, Joachin, is in an interview room. He got the crap beat out of him and almost abducted by a man."

"Shit," I swore. "I'm on my way."

I reached into my pockets and jogged out to my car. This might be the break we needed. I just hoped that Joachin was all right.

Chapter Twenty-Six

Harris

"Have you been to the hospital?" I asked Joachin while we sat in the interview room. He was stretched out on a couch with an icepack on his face. He shook his head and groaned. "Alright, well, I think maybe that you need to go. That swelling looks pretty bad, and I think you might also have a concussion."

Joachin groaned again. The door swung open, and Maverick came in looking wild. I smirked as it was the first time I'd ever seen him react to someone like that. He paid no attention to me as he went to the couch, lifted Joachin into his arms, and searched his face.

"God, this is bad," Maverick winced as he took in the misshapen swelling that was slowly taking over Joachin's side of his face. His right eye was completely swollen shut.

"I suggested we take him to the hospital."

"I agree. Did you know the man that did this?" Maverick asked.

"He has been at the club heaps of times. He tried to get me in the car. He tried to take me. Mav, is he the man that has been taking the men?"

Maverick looked over at me, and I nodded my head. "You take Joachin into the hospital. I'll take Xavier and go to the club and get footage."

"His car, he left his car. He might've returned to get it, but he ran away when the man saved me," Joachin explained through swollen lips.

"Do you remember where it was parked? And is the guy that saved you here?"

Joachin nodded his head. "Yeah, it was parked on Sandhurst Lane, and the guy was talking to another lady. He was the one that brought me in."

"Good," I said. "I'll go and find him and see if he could get a number plate at least. If the car isn't there, that will give us something to begin with. I'll get the uniform to Sandhurst Lane to see if the car is still there and, if it is, to secure it until Xavier and I get there. I'll also ring Lincoln and get him to pull whatever tapes he had of Joachin and this guy leaving."

"Thank you," Maverick said as he stood from the couch with Joachin in his arms. "Come on, Little Bit, we must get you to the hospital. I don't like the look of how much swelling is going on."

Joachin groaned and nestled his head against Maverick's shoulder. There would be time to tease Maverick later, but for now, I recognised my friend was focused on helping this man who had wormed his way out of Maverick's bed and into his heart.

I left the interview behind Maverick and watched as he carried Joachin down to the parking lot. I went to the front desk and waited for Jessie to end the call she was on.

"Hey, was that Maverick carrying a guy down the hallway?" she asked with a bemused look.

I snorted and nodded. "Yep. I think the big man has melted his heart a little."

Jessie giggled. "Good. He needs someone. The guy that brought him in is in interview room five with Michaela."

"Thanks, Jessie," I said with a smile. "Can you organise some uniform to head into Sandhurst Lane in Carlton to secure it? I don't know what kind of car they are looking for, but apparently, the perp left his car behind, and I'm hoping it's still there."

Jessie nodded her head, picked up the radio and called through the dispatch who would send out some uniforms to secure the area. If they at least blocked off the whole lane, any cars in the region could be looked at. I turned my attention to the interview room that held the witness and knocked lightly on the door before I walked in.

"Hello, my name is Detective Harris Bishop. I understand that you brought Joachin in this morning?"

The man was a short, stocky man with a balding head. He nodded. "Is the boy alright?"

"My partner has taken him to the hospital, but I think he will be alright. He was fortunate that you heard him and were able to put an end to the attack. Others, unfortunately, haven't been so lucky."

The man's eyes widened, and he gasped. "He could have been killed?"

I nodded my head. "I was wondering if I could possibly ask you some questions."

"Of course," the man said with a rapid nod.

"Great," I sat in the chair beside him. "What is your name?"

The man shook his head. "Sorry. I'm rude not introducing myself. My name is Brian Mackay."

"Nice to meet you, Brian. So, can you tell me anything about the man and his car?"

Brian nodded his head. "He was a tall guy, much taller than me and the young guy. Bulky, but not fat, more muscular. He had black hair cut in one of those trendy cuts, shaved on the sides with it long on top."

I nodded. "I do know."

Brian licked over his bottom lip. "The car is a black van, but not a van, I don't know what they are called. They sort of look like a four-wheel drive and a van cross."

"Like this?" Michaela asked as she turned her phone to Brian.

He nodded and pointed at the phone. "Yes. Just like that."

I looked at the screen and noted that he meant an SUV. "Did you happen to get the model of the car or even a number plate?"

Brian shook his head. "No. I'm sorry. I was so focused on the kid screaming. I didn't take any notice of anything else. My mind just went blank."

"That's okay. What you've given me is helpful. Thank you. Michaela, can you get Brian's statement and contact details? Then you're free to go."

"Thank you," Brian said. "I hope you get this guy before he kills someone else."

"So do I," I said. It made me nervous how close Joachin came to being killed.

Chapter Twenty-Seven

Maverick

"You know I can walk," Joachin grumbled as I carried him through the emergency doors.

"I know, but let me carry you. It makes me feel better."

Joachin didn't say anything but snuggled in closer to my chest. I would have to investigate my feelings later. I was being overprotective of this guy. I knew that probably meant a lot more about my feelings, and I would have to reassess that later, but for now, none of it mattered. All that mattered was making sure he was safe and well.

"Hi Maverick, what's going on?" Tania, the triage nurse, asked.

"This is Joachin, he was beaten last night."

"Alright, let me get a wheelchair," Tania said as she stood from the desk and moved over to the wheelchair beside the door before she pushed it toward me. I gingerly sat Joachin in the seat and stroked my fingers lightly over his hair.

"Someone did a number on you. Bring him through to the back. We don't need everyone hearing this," Tania said as she swung the door to triage open.

I wheeled Joachin through the door and parked him against the triage bed as Tania took his vital signs and blood pressure.

"How long ago did it happen?" Tania asked.

"About four this morning," Joachin mumbled. His eyes were swollen shut, and his lips were busted and huge. Blue bruising moved its way all over the right side of his face, and he had fingerprints around his throat.

"Alright, did you just get beaten, or was it a sexual assault as well?"

Joachin shook his head. "No, he just punched me and choked me."

"Okay, so we don't need to administer a rape kit?"

"No."

"Alright, let's get you back in a cubicle, and the doctor will see you. I'm assuming you will have forensics take photos and swabs?"

I nodded my head. "Yeah. I'll give Dean a ring and organise someone to come out."

Tania smiled and nodded. "Come on back this way."

We followed her into a small, isolated room with a door. It was the one they used for more delicate cases, generally rape cases and other assaults. It was a way to give the victim some privacy.

"Hop on the bed," I said to Joachin when I parked the wheelchair beside the bed.

He stood shakily and took my hand as I guided him to climb on the bed. He laid his head on the pillow, and I noticed tears begin to leak from the corner of his eyes. I stroked my hand up and down his arm.

"I should never have gone with him," Joachin cried.

"I know, baby, I know. Do you know the guy's name?"

Joachin shook his head. "I've seen him there heaps. He normally goes on a weekend. This was my first time seeing him there on a weekday."

I frowned. "Is he there when I am?"

Joachin nodded. "Yeah. I don't think you've ever talked to him, though."

My frown deepened as I thought about the men I'd seen at the Pink Flamingo. "What does he look like?"

"Tall like you. Muscly with black hair, shaved on the sides and long on top. He has tattoos up his arms."

I scratched my chin as I circulated all the guys I'd noticed. One guy kept coming to mind, and I wasn't sure if I was getting it right. If I were, Xavier would have spoken to him when we were there the other weekend. Shit, if it was him, he was right fucking there. He was a regular, and I'd seen him there often. Had he been taking guys right under my fucking nose?

It was like a punch in the gut as I thought about the number of guys that had gone missing. If it was him all along. I tried to cast my mind over the victims and if I saw any of them talking to him. I couldn't remember. It was frustrating as hell. I'd never spoken to him. He wasn't my type. I wasn't into the whole power top thing. Shit. I scrubbed my hand down over my face. This was a fucking nightmare. And here I sat with a kid whose body I could have been collecting from under another bridge.

I pulled my phone from my pocket and texted Dean, Harris and Xavier. We needed to find this bastard, and we needed to find him quick.

Chapter Twenty-Eight

Xavier

I pulled up at Sandhurst Lane and looked around. The uniform had cordoned off the entire lane, which helped keep it there. I made sure to take notice of anyone who might look a bit suspicious, but there was not really anyone around. This area of Melbourne wasn't busy during the day and only came to life at night. Even at four in the morning when Joachin was attacked was a strange hour on a weekday. But the Pink Flamingo was well known for opening early and shutting late.

"Hey George, how's it going?" I said as I approached one of the uniformed cops standing at the entrance of the laneway.

"Not bad, Xavier. Harris is already here."

I smiled and nodded in thanks as I crossed the line and walked to where Harris stood talking to John from forensics. Harris looked up and smiled as I approached.

"I'm thinking this is the car," Harris said. "It matches the description given by the witness. I'm just waiting on a call back from Michaela. She showed the witness the image to tell me whether he recognised this car."

"Great. The plates come back?"

Harris nodded his head. "Yep, a Santo Perez. Forty-four from Warburton."

"Warburton? That's a fair hike to come into the city."

Harris nodded again. "That's what I thought so too."

My phone buzzed, and I pulled it out of my pocket and read the message from Maverick. I gasped and looked over at Harris. "Have you got the licence image of Santo?"

Harris nodded and pulled the image up on his phone. "Son of a mother fucking bitch," I snarled. "That's him. That's the fucking guy I spoke to last weekend."

Harris's eyes widened, and he gasped. "I remember now. I knew he looked familiar, but I couldn't place him. Then, when his record came back clean, I thought maybe he just had a recognisable face."

"I guarantee the footage that Lincoln gets from last night will be him walking out the Pink Flamingo with Joachin."

"Yeah. Alright, let's get over there, John is just waiting for Kelly to return, and then they will organise to impound the car and go over it."

"Great," I said as I started back down the alley toward the car. I'd been speaking to this son of a bitch. He'd been right there. And he had picked us as cops. He was basically laughing in our faces. Shit. If I'd realised sooner, we could have prevented Joachin from being hurt. Damn it. But knowing that Santo lived in Warburton, an excellent seventy-five kilometres away, meant he could be anywhere. I scanned the streets again. He left his car. He'd made a colossal mistake, and that went in our favour. Now, we just had to find him.

Harris and I walked into the club and noticed the place was quiet. It wasn't quite opening time, which meant the barflies hadn't arrived yet and the bartender would still be setting up.

"Hey guys, Lincoln said to expect you," a young woman spoke as we approached the bar. "I'm Samara."

"Nice to meet you, Samara, I'm Detective Harris Bishop, and this is my colleague Detective Xavier Cooper. Was Lincoln able to get footage from last night?"

Samara nodded. "Yep. I had to show him how to do it, but I could get it onto a USB for you."

"Amazing, thank you so much," Harris said as he reached out and took the USB stick from the bartender.

"Were you able to see Joachin leaving with anyone?"

"Yeah. He is a regular here, but I don't know his name. You don't see a super clear image of him, but it was enough to be able to recognise him."

"Dark hair, big?" I asked.

Samara nodded her head. "Yeah, that's him. I really hope you get him. Joachin is an adorable kid. He doesn't deserve to be treated like that."

"We will be doing our damnedest to get him," Harris growled.

"Good."

Chapter Twenty-Nine

Harris

I wanted to be anywhere but the lawyer's office. But I'd already made the appointment last week and needed to get this sorted. However, sitting here made me feel like this was all real. My marriage was ending. This was hell. I hated it.

"Mr Bishop, would you like to follow me?" the receptionist asked.

I stood and nodded before following her down a hallway to an obnoxiously designed office that oozed wealth, from the enormous paintings on the wall and the long bookcase stuffed with legal books to the massive hardwood desk in the middle of the room.

"Mr Bishop," a tall, lanky man said as he stood to shake my hand.

"Thank you for seeing me, Michael."

He nodded his head. "It's no problem. Please have a seat."

I sat opposite the lawyer in one of the leather seats and stretched my legs. I was used to working with lawyers. Being a cop, we often had run-ins with them. But this was different. This was a lawyer trying to protect his client. This was someone that I needed to make sure my marriage ended well.

"I understand that you and your wife are filing for a formal separation." I nodded my head. Michael smiled. "Do you have an idea of what you want regarding assets?"

I sighed and shook my head. "I was happy to walk away, but Taylor said she would move out of the house. So, if she is willing, I'd like to just sell it and take half of whatever is left over after the mortgage is paid."

Michael nodded. "That makes it easy. What about furniture? Vehicles? Leisure items?"

I shook my head. "No, I've got my car, and she has hers, everything else she can have."

"Very good. Regarding the children, have you contacted child support to sort out that end of things?"

"Yeah. They are taking money from my wage and giving it straight to Taylor."

"And visitation?"

"We haven't got anything official from the courts, but Taylor agreed that I could have the kids on the weekend."

Michael smiled again. "Well, you've made my job easy. Do you need a court order, or do you think Taylor will remain reasonable regarding custody?"

I shrugged my shoulders. "I never thought she would cheat on me, so I don't know what she is capable of." I shook my head. "I don't think she will fight me on it. But if she does, then we will cross that bridge."

Michael nodded his head. "Do you know if Taylor has a lawyer?"

I shook my head again. "No, I've not spoken with her."

"That's okay, I'll be able to do all of that. If you can give me Taylor's contact details, I can find out what she wants to do from her. This is likely to get messy only if she wants more than half. However, it will be a pretty easy separation in that aspect."

I sighed and ran my hands down over my pants. At least one part of this whole mess was going to be easy. Everything else felt shit. My world was spinning out of control, and I didn't know how to bring it all together.

"It does get easier," Michael said, breaking into my thoughts.

I snorted and shook my head. "When?"

Michael smiled sympathetically. "I've been where you are. I was a cop before I was a lawyer and lost my wife the same way. This job isn't made for families, especially detectives."

I raised my brows. "Yeah. Where did you work?"

"I was part of the Drug Unit out of St Kilda."

"Shit, yeah, that wouldn't have been easy."

Michael shook his head. "No, not at all. I worked undercover and could be gone for months on a case. One day, I came home, and my house was empty. I was left with a note. So, I get it. But you do one day find it easier to deal with."

I sighed and nodded. "Thank you."

Michael winked and stood. He stuck his hand out to shake mine. "Take care of yourself, Harris. I'll ring you once I speak with Taylor and find out what is happening."

"Thank you," I said again as I shook his hand. I didn't feel any lighter or better about the situation, but it was good to know someone understood what I was going through. Now I had to shake it all off and hopefully catch us a killer.

Chapter Thirty

S anto

"Shit," I growled as I realized just how much I'd fucked up. I'd doubled back, but by the time I found the lane I'd parked in, the cops had already cordoned it off. I scrubbed my hands up over my face. Without luck, the guy and the pretty boy couldn't identify my car, but I didn't hold out hope. I had to find a way home and get the fuck out of there.

I growled as I pounded the concrete toward the train station. I'd never been so fucking sloppy. I should have stuck with my routine, but I got greedy and cocky, and now I'd fucked it all. I was fuming when I went through the ticket aisle to the train station and waited on the platform.

I stared at the timetable and saw that the train wasn't expected for another fifteen minutes. The closest I was going to be able to get to Warburton was Lilydale, which meant a bus from there. I growled again low in my throat as I moved through my mind for options to get me out of the disaster I'd created.

I'd fucked it all up. If the cops discovered my car and made it back to my place before I had a chance to get out there, I would be caught for sure.

"You alright?" a young lady said from beside me.

I narrowed my eyes and curled my lip over my top teeth. Her big blue eyes grew more expansive, and she raised her hands. "Sorry. Meant no harm."

She quickly backed away and glanced over her shoulder as she moved further down the platform. I turned my attention to the stone on the ground in front of me as I tried to think of how I would get out of it. My dog was still at the house, which would at least buy some time. They would have to call animal control to keep him under control. He would attack anyone that wasn't me going into that house. Not that it would matter; I wouldn't be able to get in and out without being noticed.

Living so far out of town was great, but the downside meant I couldn't sneak in on foot. I would be seen. I rubbed the back of my neck. I had a friend in Lilydale, but he would likely think it was weird if I just showed up at his place. I could lie and say that my car broke down. I pulled my phone from my pocket and brought up the internet as I searched for rental vehicles. This might be the one thing I could do to get away. If I could at least get across the border, I might be able to hide low for long enough to get back to the house or something.

I scanned down over the different rental places. I wanted to use one of the smaller ones. The ones that the cops were probably less likely to look at. In truth, I had no idea who they would look at. I pressed on one of the numbers and put my phone to my ear.

"Good morning, Tremble Rentals. Can I help you?"

"Yeah, I was wondering if I could rent a car for a few days?"

"Sure thing. I just have to get some information from you."

"Can I come into the office to do all this?" I interrupted.

"Oh, um, yeah," the girl on the other end replied. I could feel her unease and knew that she would likely spook and not rent to me if I didn't pull back.

"Sorry, I don't mean to be gruff; my car just broke down, and I'm frustrated."

"Of course. I understand how aggravating that is. But sure, come down, and we can go through everything here. Do you know where we are?"

"Yeah, I'll get an Uber there."

"Sure thing. See you when you get here."

I ended the call and quickly downloaded the Uber app before ordering a car for me and leaving the platform. This wasn't ideal. Once I had the car, I would have to ditch my phone and get another one. I would probably have to come up with a whole new identity.

My head was aching at the very thought of all of the shit I was going to have to do. I was angry with myself, and I hated that I'd fucked it all up. I got greedy. I let my fucking dick rule. I shook my head. That wasn't true. It wasn't my dick, it was my pride. I wanted to take what belonged to the cop. I tried to stick it to him, and I got cocky. I was an idiot and made a huge mistake.

Chapter Thirty-One

Maverick

"Have you got someone that can stay with you at home, Joachin?" the doctor asked as he stood in the hospital room.

Joachin shook his head and then groaned. "No. I'm on my own."

I frowned. I didn't know anything about this guy, which made me feel bad. I'd fucked every which way but Sunday, but I didn't even know if he had family or anything.

"You can come and stay with me," I said before suddenly thinking about what Harris would think.

Joachin tried to smile and shook his head again. "No. I don't want to be a bother. I've got some friends I can call on."

"Are you sure? You will be safe at my place."

Joachin reached out his hand. "Maverick, thank you. Having you here with me in the hospital has been enough."

I sighed and nodded. "Okay, well, at least let me drive you home."

"Okay," Joachin agreed. I wanted to ensure that he had decent people around him who would take his injuries seriously. The last thing I wanted was for him to fall into a coma and die because I didn't take the time to make sure he was safe.

"Alright then, well, I'll get the paperwork organised, and you can head home," the doctor explained before he turned and left the room.

"Do you know your friend's numbers so I can ring them and have them waiting for you?" I questioned.

Joachin hummed. "Not off by heart, but my phone is in my pocket, and their numbers are stored there."

"Do you have a passcode on your phone?" I asked as I slid his phone from his jeans pocket.

"No, just swipe up." I opened his contact list, stifling a giggle at the wallpaper of a unicorn farting rainbows.

"Who do you want me to call?"

"Lisa. She is the closest I have to a sister. She'll have a meltdown when she sees me. She hates that I go out and have one-night stands. But she will make sure I'm cared for."

I nodded and pressed Lisa's number before putting it on speakerphone and listening to it ring.

"Jo-Jo, what are you up to?" a girl chirped as she answered.

"Hi Lisa, sorry to call you like this, my name is Detective Maverick Wolfe. I'm here in the hospital with Joachin, I have you on speakerphone," I quickly explained.

"Oh god, what's happened?" Lisa exclaimed, sounding panicked.

"Joachin was attacked last night. His injuries are superficial; there is a lot of bruising and swelling, but the doctors are concerned that he might have a concussion and would like someone to be with him when he is at home."

"Shit, yeah, of course. Can Joachin hear me?"

"Yeah, I can hear you Li-Li."

"Good, come back to my place. I'll get you set up in the spare room. You are not to go back to your home. You know that it won't be any help for you there."

Joachin frowned slightly and groaned. It made me curious about what she meant. Was he not living somewhere safe?

"Okay, I'll come to yours."

"Thank you. And thank you, Detective. When can I expect you both?"

"The doctor is just finalising his discharge, and then we will be on our way."

"Great. I'll see you soon. Thank you for taking care of Joachin. He is like the little brother I never had but always wanted."

I smiled at her statement and felt warmth oozing through the phone. "I'm glad he has someone good in his life."

Lisa said goodbye and ended the call. "Joachin, what did she mean when she said your house wasn't good?"

Joachin sighed and shrugged his shoulders. "I don't exactly have a house."

"What do you mean?" I asked with a frown.

"It's a long story that I don't feel like telling. But I don't have a family. I don't have anyone apart from Lisa, but I also recognise that she has her own life and family, so I don't like to throw myself on her."

My frown deepened as I looked at him. "Are you homeless?"

Joachin snorted and shrugged his shoulders. "I have a home. It just isn't mine."

"You are talking in circles."

Joachin let out a long sigh. "I know. Maverick, you're a good guy. Way too good for what I deserve."

"What do you mean?"

Joachin gave me a tight-lipped smile but didn't say anymore. My curiosity had been piqued. I wondered more about this young man and who he was. And what made him such a bad guy. I didn't understand it. My radar was usually pretty good for picking up those that weren't good people. It never registered with Joachin. I leaned back in the chair and watched him in silence as a single tear rolled down his swollen cheek. There was so much to this guy that I didn't know, and I hated the thought that his story might have been one of horror.

Chapter Thirty-Two

X avier
"We need to wait for a search warrant," Harris growled as we sat in front of the farmhouse. From this distance, I could see the house, which looked almost abandoned.

"I don't even know if someone lives there," I mused.

Harris nodded his head. "Yeah, it's pretty rundown. I guess this is probably the best place to live if you will be a serial killer. It's out of the way, and no one will know what you do out here."

I hummed and stared along the long driveway. It had been a house out of the way, off the main road with the Yarra River running between it and the major highway that went through Warburton.

I ran my hand down over my face and yawned. "Have you heard anything from Mav yet?"

Harris nodded and looked down at his phone. "He sent me a text saying that Joachin was going to be released from the emergency room. Thankfully, it looks like all of the wounds are superficial. He was fucking lucky."

I nodded. I was furious with myself. I had this guy in my grasp. I'd spoken to him. He had picked us as cops, and I had no idea that he was the guy we were there hunting. I couldn't believe that my radar didn't go off. I usually had a pretty good clue on things like that. But he didn't ring any alarm bells at all.

"Do you reckon this bloke has come back here?" I pondered out loud.

Harris hummed. "It would be a fair effort. I was looking at public transport. He would have to catch a train to Lilydale, then a bus to

Warburton, and then walk here. I guess he could have got a taxi or an Uber."

"Maybe it is worth getting dispatch to send out his description to Uber and the taxi ranks, just in case."

"Good idea. All patrol has got his picture, but I didn't think of sending it to taxis and Uber."

Harris picked up the radio and called through, giving the order to contact the taxi directorate and Uber with the photo of the guy. We settled back in our seats and continued to watch the house. There was no movement, and even on the road, there wasn't a single person.

After sitting for around about an hour, Harris's phone rang. "Hello, Harris," he answered. He listened and nodded to the caller. His brows pulled deeper into a frown. "Okay, we are heading there now. Call the rental company, get the details on the car that he has hired and get it out to all patrol to be on the lookout."

Harris ended the call and brought the car to life. "What's going on?"

"Our perp took an Uber to a car rental place in Thomastown."

"Great," I said as Harris turned the car around and headed down the dirt road and out to the highway with lights and sirens. I hoped he would still be at the place when we arrived. However, Warburton was a long way from Thomastown, and even with lights and sirens, it would take time to get to the car rental place. I wasn't confident that we would get there in time. All I could hope is if every patrol car was on the lookout for this guy, we would soon have him.

By the time we reached the car rental, I was dismayed to see that we hadn't been able to get there on time.

"Hi guys, you must be the Detectives," a young woman with bouncy blue hair and bright eyes said as we entered the office.

"Yes," Harris said as we both held our badges to show her. "I take it that he has gone?"

The girl nodded and sighed. "Yeah, he left about thirty minutes ago. It wasn't until he left that we got the call to say that you were all looking for him. Can I ask what he is wanted for?"

"Murder," Harris answered.

The girl's eyes widened, and she gasped. "Oh my god."

"Did he happen to mention where he might be going?"

The girl shook her head. "No. He said his car broke down and needed to rent one for a few days while it got fixed."

I glanced over at Harris, who nodded his head. "Did you give dispatch the car details?"

"Yes, he rented the red Toyota Camry."

"Do they come with GPS tracking devices?" I questioned.

The girl shook her head. "No. We rent out budget cars, so most of the luxuries and added extras aren't included in our cars."

"Damn. I suspect that is why he chose you guys. If you hear from him or if he returns, can you call me directly?" Harris said as he handed the girl his card.

"Of course."

I gave her a smile and left the building. "He has about half an hour on us, and we don't know where he is going," Harris grumbled.

"There is a chance that he might return to his place to go and get things. He may not even realise that we know who he is yet, so he may go home to hide."

"Let's hope. I'll give Derek a ring and see how he's got that search warrant, and then we will get special forces on it. At the very least, we can search his place to ensure we are actually dealing with the guy we think we are."

Chapter Thirty-Three

S anto

Once in the car, I felt like I could breathe more. I continued looking into the rearview mirror to ensure I wasn't being followed. I still had no idea what I was going to do. If the cops put together my car with the pretty boy, it probably wouldn't take them long to put together that guys had been disappearing because of me. I wondered if that was a stretch. The cops had been at the club on the weekend because of men disappearing, but would they think it was me, or would they think that my attack on the pretty boy was pure coincidence?

I chewed on my bottom lip as I thought about what the hell I was going to do. They would go out to my house if I was quick. I could possibly get in and out before they had a chance to get there. It was risky. I wouldn't be able to hide the evidence. I thought about the skulls that I had lined along the shelves. I wasn't going to be able to hide them. But I might have enough time to get Rollo and leave. With somewhat of a plan, I headed for the highway that would take me to my house.

I was on edge the entire drive to Lilydale when I finally reached Yarra Glen. I continued to stare in the rear vision mirror. I'd passed a few marked cars, but none seemed to be watching me or taking any notice. I hoped that meant I would be able to get away from them.

I edged down the dirt road my house was on and leaned forward in the seat. There didn't appear to be any cars around the property. I was going to have to be quick. I pulled into my driveway and drove around the back of the house. I could hear Rollo barking the minute I pulled up, which told me someone had been there. He never got this excited if someone hadn't been to the house.

I swung the door open and stepped out of the car. "Shit," I growled as I heard the blades of a chopper. Glancing up in the sky, I saw the police helicopter approaching the house. "Fuck."

I ran for the backdoor and quickly swung it open as my mind swirled with panic. What the fuck was I going to do now. It wouldn't matter if I returned to the car and took off. If they had a chopper in the air, there would be no way to escape. I growled again and slammed my fist into the wall as anger rolled through me. Idiot. I was a fucking idiot. I fucked it up by letting my dick rule.

"Fucking idiot, faggot, cunt," I spat at myself as tears welled in my tears. I'd done everything wrong. I was fucked. Rollo sniffed at my hand and nudged my side. I sighed and scratched the top of his head. "It's over, boy."

Rollo let out a long whimper as if he understood what I was saying. I walked into my kitchen and listened to the helicopter blades circling overhead. I knew it wasn't going to be long before the house would be crawling with cops, and I would spend the rest of my life in prison. I shuddered at the thought. A place filled with people just like me. Men who pretended they didn't like other men. Men who were fucking sick in their minds, just like I was.

The tears trekked down my cheeks and dripped from my chin. I looked over at the knife block and sucked in a shuddered breath. I didn't want to spend my life around other faggots. I didn't like the temptation anymore. I didn't like this in me anymore. Before I could think about what I was doing, I reached for the knife I knew was sharp. I knew because it was what I'd used to slice up all of the bodies.

I brought the blade to my throat and swallowed hard. I closed my eyes, tears fell over my cheeks, and a sob fell from my lips. "I'm sorry, Dad," I cried. "I tried to be what you wanted. I tried not to be like this. But I couldn't control it."

The bite of the pain caused me to hiss as the blade sliced through my skin. I moved around my neck. My mouth filled with blood, and I felt it bubble up and begin to choke me. I wondered if this were what it would feel like to drown. I dropped the blade in the sink. My eyes grew heavy. My knees began to wobble. The warmth of the blood dripped down over my chest, soaking into my shirt.

My head began to spin, and dizziness filled my mind. I reached out and clasped the edge of the sink with trembling fingers. Rollo howled from beside me. I tried to reassure him, but my words sounded like gargled mumbling. My knees wobbled, and my legs wouldn't hold me up anymore. I allowed my body to collapse under its weight. My head pressed firmly against the cupboard under the sink. I sighed as the blood continued to bubble from my throat and out of my mouth. I thought I heard the sound of sirens outside and perhaps shouts. I reached out my hand to Rollo, and he lay beside me. With the last strength, I pulled myself up the sink again and took the knife. I opened my eyes enough to see Rollo.

"I'm sorry, boy," I mumbled through gargled bubbles. I couldn't let him live without me. It was cruel. I plunged the knife with all of my might into his neck. Rollo screamed in pain but laid his head beside me. I closed my eyes and let the knife drop to my side.

Darkness sucked me under, and I smiled. It was over. I was done.

Chapter Thirty-Four

Maverick

"Alright, thanks," I said as I ended the call. I'd dropped Joachin to his friend Lisa's home. She had met us on the front doorstep and looked terrified when she saw the state of his face. I helped to put Joachin in the spare bedroom and gave her the paperwork from the doctor. Lisa seemed to be an excellent friend. She fussed over Joachin and told me how scared she had been about his living situation. I didn't ask as I didn't feel that it was my place, but I was curious.

Harris had rang me on the way out to say they had a lead on the killer. His name was Santo Perez, a forty-four-year-old man from Warburton. Apparently, he'd hired a car, and Harris told me he'd returned to his house. That was where I was headed.

The phone buzzed again, and I saw that it was Xavier calling. "Maverick," I answered.

"Hey, Mav, sorry to ring again. We aren't quite at the house yet, But they've got sights on Santo from the sky. A uniform is rolling in along with the TRT. They are waiting for us with the search warrant. We aren't sure what to expect from this guy, so we want to send Tactical in first."

"Good idea," I said. "I'm about ten minutes out."

"We are just pulling into the road now. See you when you get here."

The call ended, and I pushed harder on the accelerator. My belly twisted with nerves. We didn't know what to expect from this guy. We presume that he had killed already eighteen men, and we know that he beat the hell out of Joachin. I believe that Joachin would have been his nineteenth kill had the witness not intervened. Joachin had been lucky.

I was glad that he came out of it alive. I knew I would have to examine my feelings toward Joachin at another stage. I never felt like this about anyone. I wasn't sure if it was because we had fucked, and now seeing him as a victim was muddling everything up in my head or what it was. But be damned if he hadn't managed to burrow into my cold heart. God, would my father have laughed at that. Before he died, I'd told him that I was a confirmed bachelor for life.

I finally pulled down the dirt road. There were police units everywhere. The helicopter still circled in a swoop around the house. The house was a big, sprawling farmhouse with rolling paddocks surrounding it. There were large sheds at the back of the property, but there was nothing that really hid it from the outside world. Other than the fact that it was found down a dirt road. I pulled the car up beside Harris's and stepped out.

"Hey," I greeted Harris as I came to stand beside him and Xavier.

"Hey, so, uniformly said they heard a dog yelping loudly earlier, but it has gone quiet. Tactical tried to call out to him, but there was no response," Harris explained.

"Laying low?"

Harris shrugged his shoulders. "I don't know."

Brandon came over to where we stood and shook my hand. "Hi, Mav, we are getting ready to breach entry. The guys around the back have said they could see the dog, and it looks down. I think there is a good chance the guy is down too." I frowned and nodded my head. "We are masking up and going to go in with flashbangs, just to be safe."

Flashbangs were a pepper spray bomb. As much as they were fantastic when subduing perps, it wasn't ideal as it left a residue on everything, which meant that any potential evidence could be lost. I didn't like it, but there was no way I would send the team in blind.

"Alright, we will wait for the flash to subside, and then we will follow you in."

"We've got him. He's down," a voice came over the radio.

Brandon's eyes widened, and he lifted his radio. "Give me more."

"Kitchen, I can see him through the window. He is covered in blood."

"Alright, get ready to breach," Brandon answered as he jogged to the front door.

Harris, Xavier and I followed behind. After a quick shout, the tactical team broke through the doors simultaneously and moved through the house, clearing each room. I moved to the back of the house where the kitchen was situated and saw a man I recognised lying on the floor.

"Son of a bitch," I snarled down at the dead body at my feet.

"Same guy?" Xavier asked.

"Yep. Same fucking guy, I've been at the Pink Flamingo every time he was there."

"Um, guys, we've got something you might need to see," one of the tactical members said.

Harris, Xavier and I turned to follow the team member into what appeared to be some kind of weird, kinky office space.

"Jesus," Harris exclaimed.

My eyes widened as I took in what was sitting on the shelves before us. Human skulls, all neatly lined up along the shelf. All had been thoroughly cleaned off the meat. Some of you could see the fractures that I assumed happened during the attack. While others looked reasonably intact.

"We will need forensics to bag all this up when they come. Don't touch anything," I instructed as I left the room.

"Mav, there were nineteen skulls there," Xavier said.

My eyes widened, and I gasped. "There is still a body we haven't found."

Xavier nodded his head. "Shit," Harris spat as he shook his head.

I scrubbed my hand down over my face. We had no idea of knowing who the last skull belonged to and where he fits in the timeline of murders. Until we found the guy's body, there was possibly no telling who he was.

Chapter Thirty-Five

Harris

I looked down at the body of the guy who handled nineteen deaths and one assault. He'd been right under our noses that night at the club, and none of us had picked up on it. I'd seen him talking to Xavier, and while I looked at him suspiciously, nothing raised any red flags. I glanced at Maverick as I thought about the day I'd rocked up on his doorstep. One of my best friends, well really my only best friend now that Jason had betrayed our friendship. He could have been one of the skulls that sat on the macabre shelf in what could only be described as a room of death. Hanging from the walls were all sorts of contraptions that looked like they could only be used for torture.

I scrubbed my hand down over my face. It was a complete waste of life, and what was worse, we didn't have any answers for the family as to why. I had no idea if these were hate crimes or whether he was some kind of weird kink master who got off on death. There were no answers because he was lying dead with his throat gashed open.

"We've bagged up all of the evidence in the office," Kelly said from behind me.

I turned and nodded my head. "Anything other than the skulls?"

Kelly's cheeks tinted pink, and she nodded her head. "Yeah. He had some, um, interesting taste."

I raised a brow and cocked my head to the side. "Interesting tastes?"

Kelly chuckled and nodded again. "Yeah. I've left it all for you guys to look at, but he has a load of diaries in there, and I have a feeling that might explain a bit of the why."

I smiled, and that was precisely what I'd hoped to find. We hadn't been able to prevent the guys from being murdered, but if we could give the families some answers, that would be better than nothing.

"Are you going to be able to get the DNA of the skulls to match the bodies?"

"Yep. We can take DNA from the teeth. Then, I can match each skull. I'll be able to find which is the extra one, and hopefully, we will be able to either find a match through ancestry or have his DNA on file."

"I hope so," I said with a sigh. The thought that there was another body out there somewhere and possibly a family missing their son or brother. Not that we'd received any new missing reports for anyone missing from the Pink Flamingo. That didn't necessarily mean anything, though. There was a good chance that the family might not have known that was where he was last seen. Not all guys were open with their family and friends about what they did on the weekend.

"Alright, well, I'm going to get these back, Dean will be here soon to pick up the body, and I think animal control will be taking the body of the dog."

"Thanks, Kelly."

Kelly waved her hand as she exited through the back door. I looked down again at the dead man who lay beside his dog in a pool of their combined blood. Such a damned waste of life. I had no idea if this man had family that might miss him. I assumed he probably didn't if he proudly displayed his kills on a shelf. I didn't imagine that too many people would come to visit with him.

I entered the office, where Xavier and Maverick searched the rest of the shelves and boxes.

"What have you been able to find out?"

"This was a very fucking confused man," Xavier said with a sad shake of his head.

"Yeah?"

Xavier nodded. "He was gay, but from what he writes in his journals, he was made to feel that it was evil and he should hate gay men. I think that's why he targeted gay men. It is like he was trying to appease some unseen force or something."

"So, a religious zealot?"

Xavier shook his head. "I don't think. I think this is more a kid that was possibly beaten down and broken by a homophobic family, and it fucked with his head."

"Damn. It seems like such a waste."

"It fucking is," Maverick growled. "It's a fucking waste of life. He ended these young men's lives because he hated a part of him and didn't understand that there was nothing wrong with him." I wondered if Maverick's anger was because of Joachin's injuries. He slammed a box on the desk. "I can't fucking look at this shit. It makes me sick."

I looked over his shoulder into the box and frowned. There were pictures of a dark-haired, olive-skinned boy with the saddest eyes. His face was bruised and swollen. His lips split, and bruises dotted over his bare torso. A tall man stood beside him with a snarl on his face. He posed the boy like some kind of trophy.

"You reckon that is Santo's father?"

Maverick nodded his head. "Yeah. On the back, there are letters to his father begging for forgiveness and swearing to kill off all gay men."

"Jesus. He needed help."

Maverick sighed. "His fucking father needed to be buried. I'm so over this case."

I reached out and squeezed Maverick's shoulder. "Do you think you need to perhaps step back a little?"

Maverick looked up at me, and I saw the sadness in his eyes as he nodded. "It's fucked me up. Seeing Joachin bruised and battered, knowing that he could have been one of those skulls on the shelf. Fuck, man." Maverick's voice broke, and his eyes welled with tears.

I nodded and pulled him into a tight hug. "I think someone is in love," I whispered.

Maverick threw his head back and barked out a loud laugh. He shook his head but didn't respond. The tension fell from his shoulders, and he smiled up at me. "Thanks, man. Let's wrap this up. I'm ready for a less emotional one."

"Is that even a thing?" Xavier asked over his shoulder.

I snorted and shook my head. "In this job? Highly unlikely."

Chapter Thirty-Six

Maverick

"Uncle Mav," Daisy cried as she ran into the house and flew into my arms.

"Hey there, Princess, have you come to stay with me and Dad for the weekend?"

Daisy bounced her head up and down. Her blonde curls were growing longer each time I saw her. To know that it wasn't that long ago that she was completely bald. She didn't even have eyelashes due to the chemotherapy and radiation therapy she had been through.

Imogen entered the house, and her face lit up with delight when she saw me. I held my other arm and scooped her into my chest before kissing her cheek. I looked forward to having the girls over as much as Harris. It had been a hell of a few weeks. The case was finally behind us; Joachin was now living permanently with Lisa, and his wounds had healed. I had taken a few days off. It was a much-needed break. I'd been surprised at how much this case had taken out of me.

"So, what are our plans for the weekend?" I asked as I placed the girls down. Over the last few weeks, we'd sorted out the spare room I'd used as an office, which I didn't use, and turned it into a bedroom for the girls. I'd gone over the top and filled it with toys and loads that I knew they loved. Of course, Harris told me off, but who else could I spoil.

Joachin and I had spent some time together but soon realised there was nothing between us. While it was a fun time, we were at very different places in our lives. And I wasn't in a position to take on a relationship. I watched what a disaster was left behind when a marriage ended because of the work.

Harris and Taylor had been amicable, but that didn't mean it was easy. The house was still up for sale, but Taylor and the girls had moved in with Jason. Of course, that had been an objective point of contention for Harris. It killed him to go to Jason's house to pick up the girls. I'd offered to do it, but he said he would have to get used to it. I had no idea if they had spoken since it all came out. Harris was a better man than me. I don't think I could have even looked at the guy again, let alone go to his house and pretend to be nice to him.

"Thor," Daisy called, drawing my attention back to them. I realised I'd tuned out. Harris came into the living room and talked to Imogen as they sat on the couch. Daisy was crawling along the floor with Thor by her side as the big cat smooched up to her.

"Did anyone tell me what we planned to do this weekend?" I asked.

Daisy giggled, and Imogen rolled her eyes. "Just for like the last five minutes."

I gasped and looked at Harris. "When did you get such a sassy puss?"

Harris snorted. "She's almost a teenager, you know."

My eyes widened further. "Nope. No way. Not allowed."

Imogen rolled her eyes dramatically again. "I'm going to be eleven in April."

"Stop it," I gasped. "Eleven. I mean, you're going to be moving out soon, going off to university, oh god, you're going to get married." I shook my head again and folded my arms across my chest dramatically. "I repeat, no way, not allowed."

Daisy giggled hysterically and looked over at her sister, who smirked. I could see the humour in her eyes despite her trying desperately to keep up the tedious teen act.

"Okay, okay, so we will be watching Bluey?" I asked, teasing her further.

Imogen dramatically slapped her forehead and shook her head before looking at her father with exasperation. "How do you put up with him?"

Harris barked out a laugh. "Trust my Immy, it's not easy."

I reached over to the couch and pulled her into a tight hug. "You love me."

Imogen squealed and made a show of fighting to get away from me, but I also felt the way she held me tighter. This kid was going through a tumultuous time for any kid, but add to that the changes being thrown at her, and she was underneath the sass and fire, a scared little girl.

"Alright, alright, so a Taylor Swift party?"

Imogen's eyes widened, looking up at me with a beaming smile. "You know Taylor Swift?"

"Oh honey," I cried. "I'm a Swifty."

Imogen looked over at her shoulder at Harris, who nodded his head. "Don't get him started. He has every album she has ever written."

"Seriously?"

"Oh yeah. I even learned how to make those bracelets because I knew you two liked her, so we could make some together. I know that a girl will turn eleven next month and that Taylor Swift is coming to Melbourne. When was it again?"

"In September," Imogen said.

I nodded. "That's right. In September. And well, I was going to wait until your birthday, but I suppose you can have them now."

Imogen frowned, but I could see her excitement mounting. I went to my fridge, where I'd printed out the tickets. I returned to the living room and handed her one and one to Daisy. Imogen read over the paper, and her eyes widened before she let out a high-pitched squeal.

"Oh my god," she cried. "You got us tickets?"

I chuckled and nodded. "I did. I figured you both needed something to celebrate."

Imogen wrapped her arms around me before turning to her father and wrapping her arms around his neck. "Thank you, Uncle Mav," she said.

I winked. "You're very welcome. I also bought Dad and me some tickets to take you."

"Oh Christ," Harris moaned, making me laugh. I knew he couldn't stand pop music, but I also knew he'd do anything for those little girls, so he would happily put up with the music for the night.

Daisy grinned. "I get to come to?"

"You sure do, Daisy girl."

She stood and cuddled me and cuddled her father. "Thank you."

"You're both welcome. Now, how about we have some pancakes for lunch and then start making some bracelets?"

Chapter Thirty-Seven

Harris

"Alright, the good news is that the house has sold," Michael said as we sat in his office. It had been three weeks since we'd put the house on the market. So far, the situation was working. I would pick the girls up every weekend and spend the weekend with Maverick. I was waiting for the house to sell to get my own place. Maverick didn't mind me living there, but I didn't want to overstay my welcome.

"Yeah, the real estate agent contacted me yesterday."

"Great. So, the new owners have agreed to the short settlement, so we can separate the finances in thirty days. Once the mortgage is paid off, you and Taylor will each have seventy-eight thousand each. How has custody been going?"

I nodded. It wasn't enough to buy a new house outright, but I could use the money as a deposit and get a place to suit the kids and myself. "It's been going good. Taylor has been happy for me to have the girls every weekend, and my work is happy for me to take weekends off so I can be with them."

"Fantastic. How is everything else going?"

I shrugged my shoulders. "I'm doing okay. We haven't long finished a pretty rough case that was close to my partner, so it's nice to start looking at some of the cold cases."

"Good. Alright, Harris, I won't need to see you again until the settlement ends, and then we will finish the finances. You should be good to go. It won't be anything that is needed to be done until the divorce paperwork."

I smiled and stood, holding my hand out to shake Michael's. He'd made this whole process so much easier to deal with. I didn't know how I would have been able to go through all of this without his help, Maverick, and Derek. Mav and Derek made it possible to keep me emotionally stable. It still killed me to think about Taylor and Jason's betrayal without hurting. It didn't make me as angry anymore, but it still fucking killed me.

I had kept putting off speaking to Jason, but I knew that there was going to have to be a day when I confronted him to heal. I had to bite the bullet and do it. Taylor and the girls were living with him, and the girls, while they tried not to speak about him, still did. I couldn't expect them to avoid the topic of him. I had to face the facts. He was part of their life now.

I'd texted him before meeting with Michael to organise catching up at a bar. He'd said he would talk, but I was not looking forward to it. I'd considered asking Maverick to come with me in case I got angry and tried to kill him. But it had to happen.

I walked into the bar with a heavy heart. I glanced around the room and saw Jason sitting at the bar, staring down into his pot of beer. I breathed in deeply and slowly let it out. The last time I'd seen him, we had been having a family barbecue. He'd stood beside me, laughed, and chatted as if nothing was going on. I kept looking back over the last few months to see if I could find evidence I'd ignored. But I hadn't seen anything. I'd missed everything entirely.

I walked over to Jason and slid onto the stool beside him. The bartender smiled over at me. "Just a coke, thanks," I ordered before putting my card on the bar. I didn't look at Jason until the bartender brought me my drink and returned my card.

"Look, Harris," Jason started.

I shook my head. "Don't. I don't want to hear false apologies. I don't want any of that. I only want to know one thing, why?"

Jason sucked in a deep breath and let it out as he searched my face. "I don't know." He shook his head. "It wasn't something I had ever intended to do. Fuck man, I never wanted to do something that destroyed our friendship."

"And yet you did."

Jason nodded. "Yeah, I did."

"Did you even at once consider coming and telling me? Even before you started fucking my wife? While I was sitting watching my daughter going through chemotherapy and radiation therapy, wondering every day whether she was going to die, didn't you ever think that maybe you should tell me?"

Jason nodded again. "I did. The first time Taylor and I did anything, I wanted to come to you and tell you. The guilt was killing me."

"But you never said anything. You came to my house, shared my food and my drinks, sat by my side and said nothing," I growled. I swallowed hard as the anger inside me began to rise.

"I was ashamed. If I kept it completely separate, I wouldn't hurt you. Taylor was hurting. She felt like you weren't there for her."

"How much more could I be there for her, Jason? I was in the fucking hospital with my daughter. I took the girls out to give her space as often as possible. I would hold her when she cried. I had to work, we had bills to pay, Daisy's medical bills alone meant I couldn't quit my job."

"I know. I get that. I'm sorry, Harris. I am. I handled this like a dick. What I did was wrong. I should never have fucking done it."

"But you're not going to stop," I snorted with a head shake. If he felt so fucking ashamed, he would walk away and tell Taylor to go back to me and make our marriage work. But he wasn't doing that. Instead, he moved my wife and daughters in with him and lived like they were always a family.

"You're right. Harris. I don't know what to tell you."

I shook my head. "Don't say anything. Just don't fuck with my girls. Treat them right, and we won't have a problem. But our friendship will never be more than that."

I stood without even touching my drink before I turned and walked away. I didn't know what I'd hoped for, but it hadn't made me feel better. I wasn't sure if I'd hoped he would grovel and tell me he would end things with Taylor, but it was done. I had to move on. I needed to heal and live my life differently.

I'd never been with anyone other than Taylor. I wasn't in a hurry to find anyone else. But it would be nice to learn to be independent and live for myself for a little bit. Of course, I would continue being my best dad to my girls. I would eventually heal, and I was sure the bitterness and anger I felt now would eventually dissipate. Now, it was time for me.

Epilogue

Xavier

"Hey, Mav," I said as I walked into the serial killer unit where Maverick and Harris were busy looking over files.

Maverick looked up and smiled. "What's up?"

I sat down in the chair opposite him. "I just got a call from Kelly, and she was finally able to match all of the skulls from the Pink Flamingo cases."

"Excellent," Maverick responded.

"What about the extra one?" Harris asked.

I nodded. "Yep. She finally found a match to who it is, but so far, his body hasn't been found, so I'm working on it with her, but we may never find it."

Maverick scrunched up his nose. "Damn. Who was it?"

"His name was Pablo Shanoda, a twenty-two-year-old International student from Spain."

"Was he reported missing?"

I nodded. "Yeah, his school friends had reported him, but there was a thought that maybe he had taken off. He was in his final year at university and would have to return to Spain. He was talking about not wanting to return, so they thought maybe he had disappeared. Police briefly looked for him, but there was no report of him ever attending the Pink Flamingo, so he wasn't linked. From the enquiries I did after Kelly was able to find him, his uni friends hadn't even realised he was gay."

Maverick sighed. "That's why they would never have thought he was at the Pink Flamingo."

"Where does he fit in the timeline?" Harris asked.

"Pablo went missing right before Joachin's attack, which could be why we haven't found the body yet. It was so recent."

"How did Kelly get his DNA matched?" Maverick asked.

I chuckled. "That woman is a fucking genius. Apparently, Pablo was studying medicine at university, and they had done DNA testing as part of the course. When his DNA didn't come up in the system or on ancestry, she took the chance and contacted the university labs to see if they had his DNA on record. Apparently, they keep all of their DNA on file at their labs. That was when it turned up."

"Damn. She's worth her weight," Maverick laughed.

"That she is. Anyway, I've been in contact with Pablo's family, which was fun and games. His brother could translate for us, but it was still a bit of a nightmare over the phone. Pablo's brother is coming to Australia to help with the investigation, but I'm unsure what it can do. Of course, they will want to return his head to Spain." I shook my head. "It seems so fucking sad to only be able to say, here is the coffin of your son and brother, but don't open it because there is literally only a skull in there."

"The whole damned case was such a waste of life. It showed just how much we have to change society to be more accepting," Maverick sighed.

I nodded. I thought about my own partner, Claudia. She was transgendered. If even a lot of my colleagues knew that, they would possibly ostracize me. But to commit murder for homophobic views. It disgusted me.

"What are you guys working on now?" I questioned, changing the subject.

"Well, Maverick decided to chuck us out of the frying pan and into the damned fire," Harris growled, making Maverick laugh.

I looked at Maverick with confusion. "Let's just say that the Pink Flamingo case was easy compared to this one?"

My eyes widened, and I gasped. "Damn. What is it?"

"You know the politician Martin O'Folley?"

I nodded my head. "I've heard of him."

"Yeah, Greens Senator, full of attitude and ready to cause a scene wherever he goes," Harris grumbled.

Maverick nodded his head. "Well, his nephew has gone missing while he was on holiday here in Melbourne. He was with a few friends, and they've all disappeared."

"Shouldn't this be a missing person's unit case?" I questioned.

Maverick shook his head. "Typically, it would be. Especially when it is a group of guys that go missing like this, we might assume they got pissed and are sleeping it off somewhere, but with it being Martin O'Folley's nephew, Derek wanted us to handle it. If they turn up alive and hungover, then that is good."

"How long have they been missing?"

"Two days."

I hummed. "That's not really that unusual for a group of guys going out on a bender holiday."

Maverick nodded. "I agree. I suspect we are going to find them holed up in a hotel somewhere hungover and probably coming down off whatever pills they popped."

I sighed and tapped my knuckles on the table in front of me. "Well, good luck with that one man."

Harris laughed. "You're just happy you don't have to work this one."

"You're right," I agreed before I wiggled my fingers in a wave and walked out of the office. One thing I could guarantee was that murders kept happening, so while I wasn't working the case of a senator's missing nephew, I knew that there was going to be another one coming my way. As if Derek was psychic and could read my mind, he stepped out of his office and waved me over.

"Hey Xav, we've got a body. A young girl looks like she's been raped and strangled by a home intrusion."

I groaned. "Okay, I'll get on it."

Derek smiled. "Thank you. Talk to you soon."

I waved and headed toward the door. And just like that, I was going to investigate the snuffed-out life of one more person. Humans were assholes.

The End

Don't miss out!

Visit the website below and you can sign up to receive emails whenever Samuel Davies publishes a new book. There's no charge and no obligation.

https://books2read.com/r/B-A-MQKW-TPGXE

BOOKS 2 READ

Connecting independent readers to independent writers.

Did you love *Kiss of Death*? Then you should read *Just A Joke*[1] by S L Davies!

[2]

Sarah was a silent girl. People didn't understand. They said because she could talk, she should. But it wasn't that simple for Sarah; she couldn't speak, and her tongue wouldn't work to form the words when she wanted to. The words wouldn't come out. As a result, Sarah was bullied by her peers; she had no friends.

But when her only companion, her mother, dies, Sarah's life becomes in turmoil. Suddenly she finds herself thrust into a world she doesn't understand. One that is filled with pain, anguish and fear. However, when Sarah stumbles across Kai and Justin, she knows she can face everything, including Jett and Valentino.

This is a dark story with some potentially triggering themes.

---

1. https://books2read.com/u/49drXd

2. https://books2read.com/u/49drXd

Read more at https://www.amazon.com/~/e/B0832T8F7Z.

Also by Samuel Davies

On The Hunt
On The Hunt
Always Watching
Retirement Killer
Morgue
Kiss of Death

About the Author

Samuel Davies is a crime author living in Australia.

www.ingramcontent.com/pod-product-compliance
Lightning Source LLC
Chambersburg PA
CBHW071317130726
47996CB00002B/516